Vampire Hollows
(Kiera Hudson Series One)
Book 5

Tim O'Rourke

ISBN: 10:1478375655
ISBN-13:978-1478375654

Copyright 2012 by Tim O'Rourke

Story Editor
Lynda O'Rourke
Book cover designed by:
Carles Barrios
Copyright: Carles Barrios 2011
Carlesbarrios.blogspot.com
Edited by:
Carolyn M. Pinard
carolynpinardconsults@gmail.com
www.thesupernaturalbookeditor.com

For my friend Richard Ayres
The tall guy with a big heart & his cat Dave

More books by Tim O'Rourke

Vampire Shift (Kiera Hudson Series 1) Book 1
Vampire Wake (Kiera Hudson Series 1) Book 2
Vampire Hunt (Kiera Hudson Series 1) Book 3
Vampire Breed (Kiera Hudson Series 1) Book 4
Wolf House (Kiera Hudson Series 1) Book 4.5
Vampire Hollows (Kiera Hudson Series 1) Book 5
Dead Flesh (Kiera Hudson Series 2) Book 1
Dead Night (Kiera Hudson Series 2) Book 1.5
Dead Angels (Kiera Hudson Series 2) Book 2
Dead Statues (Kiera Hudson Series 2) Book 3
Dead Seth (Kiera Hudson Series 2) Book 4
Dead Wolf (Kiera Hudson Series 2) Book 5
Dead Water (Kiera Hudson Series 2) Book 6
Witch (A Sydney Hart Novel)
Black Hill Farm (Book 1)
Black Hill Farm: Andy's Diary (Book 2)
Doorways (Doorways Trilogy Book 1)
The League of Doorways (Doorways Trilogy Book 2)
Moonlight (Moon Trilogy) Book 1
Moonbeam (Moon Trilogy) Book 2
Vampire Seeker (Samantha Carter Series) Book 1

Chapter One

The truck lunged to the right, then to the left, and I nearly lost my footing. Doctor Hunt reached out to steady me and I snapped my arm away.

"Get off!" I hissed.

"Kiera?" he asked, his eyes growing wide. "What's wrong?"

"I know who you are!" I shouted, raising my claws as to defend myself should he try and grab for me again. *"You're Elias Munn!"*

The truck continued to rattle, lurch, and bump, and I pressed the flat of my hand against its frame to keep my balance.

"I'm not..." Hunt started and I jabbed at him with my free hand, fingernails long, black and curved.

"You're behind everything," I spat. "You're the invisible man
we've all been searching for!"

"What?" Hunt cried in disbelief. "You can't really believe that?"

"Why not?" I asked, staring into his eyes, trying to see something – *anything*. "It all makes sense now!" But did it? I couldn't work it out. Where did Hunt fit into all of this? With my mind racing back to my days of training, I frantically tried to search for opportunity and motive. But did any of those rules apply to him? Wasn't Elias Munn a twisted killer who only wanted the destruction of the human race because he had been spurned by his true love?

"I see it in your eyes, Kiera," he said, his voice softer now.

"See what?" I shouted.

"Your uncertainty," he said back. "Why would I help you escape from that zoo if all I wanted was to kill you anyway?"

"Because you need me to love you," I replied.

With a half-smile on his lips, Hunt looked at me and said, "I'm flattered, Kiera, but aren't I a little bit old for you?"

"I'm not talking about us being lovers!" I barked at him, my right claw still held out before me. "I could love you as a friend, as a father! And by you helping and taking care of me, there would be a very good chance I could grow emotionally attached to you – love you perhaps."

"That wasn't my reason for helping you, Kiera," he shouted back over the roar of the truck's engine. "I want this Elias Munn dead as much as you. I lost my wife because of him and almost Kayla and Isidor too!"

"So if you're not Munn, why were you trying to escape that facility with my mother, Phillips, and Sparky? Why have your head covered? Who were you trying to hide your identity from?"

"*They* were trying to hide my identity from you!" Hunt said.

"And why would they want to do a thing like that?"

"Because they were using me as a decoy, for crying out loud!" Hunt insisted.

"A decoy?" I asked confused.

"They wanted you to think that I was this Elias Munn, so you would follow me while the real Munn got away," he started to explain. "They covered my head because if you had seen it was me, you would never have followed. You would've smelled a rat and not come after us." Then, looking at me he added, "But then again, perhaps you have come after me, not to save me, but because you did believe that I was Munn."

I looked at him and could see despair in his blue eyes. It was as if they had clouded over like a summer sky that was threatening a storm.

"So if you're not this Elias Munn, who is?" I asked with a sneer, but something in my heart told me perhaps he was telling the truth. "You must have some idea. You told Murphy back at the Hallowed Manor that you had your suspicions."

"I can't be certain, but..." he started.

"But what?" I demanded.

Before he could answer me, the truck tipped onto its side and I toppled backwards onto my arse, my arms and legs pin wheeling. Hunt was up, throwing away the cloak he had draped over his shoulders. He came towards me, his hand outstretched. I threw my hands up, as if to protect myself from him.

Hunt could see the fear in my eyes as he came towards me. Then reaching out, he grabbed hold of me and yanked me to my feet.

"Kiera, I'm not going to hurt you. You've got to trust me," he said, his eyes fixed on mine.

Pushing his hand away, I looked at him and said, "Who then? Who is this Elias Munn?"

"Who is it that you love?" he asked, and his face looked almost sad.

"What...why?" I stammered as I searched my feelings. I knew in my heart that I had only ever loved a very few people. My father, mother, and if I were to be honest with myself, I knew I had fallen in love with...

The roof of the truck was suddenly ripped open as a set of claws shot into the darkness of the cargo hold and yanked Hunt out. I looked up to see his feet disappearing through the jagged hole. Leaping from the back of the truck, I swept up into the sky through the snow that continued to fall like giant feathers.

With my wings poised on either side of me, I snapped my head left and right and stared through the snow and into the night. Narrowing my eyes to slits, I saw a dark shadow whisk upwards and away. Pressing my arms against my sides, and tilting my head back like the shape of an arrow, my wings instinctively spread open, and with those little black fingers seeming to grab at the air, I propelled myself forward. I tore through the snowy air as I made my way towards the black-winged shape that was racing away from me. My long hair bellowed out behind me, and I could hear and feel the wind pressing itself against me as I cut through it. I don't know how fast I was flying, but when I dared to glance down, the treetops and barren moors below me were just a blur.

I gained on the shape ahead of me, and as I drew closer to it, I could see Doctor Hunt struggling with the creature that had snatched him away. Hunt kicked and lashed out at the Vampyrus, but the other seemed stronger. In a flicker of shadows, the Vampyrus ripped and tore at Hunt. Over the sound of the roaring wind, I heard a cry that almost froze my heart. It was an ear-splitting scream of utter agony. Then I watched in horror as Hunt fell from the Vampyrus' claws and dropped from the sky, his own wings fluttering on either side of him like two torn sails.

His attacker seemed to hover just beneath a grey belly of swollen cloud. Whoever it was looked back at me, and I looked into their face, but like in my dreams – *nightmares* – his face was a blur of shadows that appeared to twist and contort before my very eyes. Blinking, I looked back but he had gone, disappearing into the cloud that lumbered across the night sky, showering the earth below in snow.

I looked down and could see Hunt spiralling towards the ground. Twisting around in the sky, I shrugged my shoulders to spread my wings and I shot down after him. The ground raced up towards me at a terrifying rate. Still not really sure how to use the two glistening wings, I hoped that I would know how to stop in time. Reaching out with my claws, I snatched at Hunt as I shot past him. Then, knowing that I had just seconds to catch him before we both smashed into the hard, rocky ground of the moors, those bony black fingers at the tips of my wings, which had once repulsed me so much, gripped hold of Hunt. Seeing that I had caught him, I arched my back and came to a sudden stop, just inches from the ground. I floated downwards, placing my boots gently against the earth. Hunt felt heavy and lifeless. Placing him out of the blizzard, I rested him against a large rock and he slumped forward.

"Doctor Hunt!" I roared over the howling wind. "Who is Elias Munn?"

Gently taking his face in my hands, I lifted his head to look at him. His eyes were open and they stared back at me. Snow fell onto his black hair and chest. Staring into his eyes, I knew there was no life in them, but I didn't want to accept that. Hunt had just been about to tell me who Elias Munn was, I didn't want him to go – not yet.

"Please tell me," I whispered into his face. "I need to know." But he just looked back at me, his mouth drawn into a permanent grimace, like a gash across his face.

Then I noticed the snow that covered his chest and lap had turned pink, then red, almost black. With one of my claws, I brushed the snow away and closed my eyes at the sight of the ragged hole in the centre of his chest where his heart had been removed.

Laying him down, I stood up, clenching my claws. I then threw my head back and screamed into the wind.

Chapter Two

I wept as I covered Hunt's body with some branches and leaves from a nearby crop of trees. They weren't just tears of sadness for him, they were more tears of frustration. It didn't seem fair. However close I got to Elias Munn, the further he seemed to move away. Murphy had said that the invisible man – Munn – always seemed to be several steps ahead of us. It was like we had been chasing a ghost, something made of smoke; someone made of vapour.

When his identity was close to being revealed, it was snatched away from me, just like Hunt had been snatched away from the truck. As I gently placed the broken branches over Hunt's body, I thought back to what he had said to me just before he had been taken and murdered.

Who is it that you love? He had said.

But what kind of love? How deep does this so-called love have to be? I loved my mother and father, and on some level, I loved Kayla and Isidor like a brother and sister. But I knew there were two others I cared deeply about and one of them I had fallen in love with. I couldn't deny that to myself any longer, because if I did, then perhaps I would fail to see Elias Munn's true identity.

Standing, I looked down at Hunt's covered body and watched as the giant snowflakes seesawed down, smothering his makeshift grave like a blanket.

I turned away and headed back in the direction from where I had come. My wings trailed behind me, and reaching out, I ran the tips of my claws over their black glittering surface. They felt like the softest of feathers – like silk somehow, but tougher. The three bony fingers at the tip of each wing were curled closed like a deformed-looking fist. I looked at them and imagined them open, and no sooner had I conjured the thought in my head, the fingers curled open like the petals of a black rose. I pictured them closed and they folded inwards on themselves. It was no harder for me to open and close them than it was my own hands. I looked back at my wings. Now that they were out, how did they go away again? Just like I had done with those bony black fingers, I just imagined them gone again, and before I knew what was happening, my shoulders were rolling forward as if I were shrugging and the wings were withdrawing back inside of me. It wasn't a painful feeling, just uncomfortable. I could feel them wrapping themselves around my ribcage, and for just a few moments, I felt short of breath. It was like my lungs were being squeezed or filled with warm water. Then the feeling was gone and I could breathe again, and I felt no different than I had for the last twenty years of my life. I looked down at my hands, which didn't really look like hands anymore. They were more of a cross between a crow's claw and that of an eagle. The skin covering my hands had taken on an almost translucent look, like marble. My fingers were longer – way longer than normal. I held them up before me and I guessed my middle finger was somewhere between ten and twelve inches long. Each one of them was capped with a sharp, black fingernail which was slightly hooked. I looked at them and wished that they would go, and no sooner had the thought entered my head, the claws were shrinking away and leaving behind my normal-sized fingers. I imagined the claws again, and they were back in an instant like blades being sprung from a flick-knife. I wished them away and they went as quickly as they had appeared. I still wasn't happy or sure about the changes that my body was making and the thought of those little black fingers curled around my ribcage still made me feel sick, but the claws? They were pretty cool.

Running my tongue gently over my front teeth, I could feel that my canines were longer and sharper than before. With the tip of the thumb on my right hand, I pushed gently against one of them, then, snapped it away as it pierced the flesh. Blood ran down the length of my thumb and trailed around my wrist. My first instinct was to mop it up with my tongue, but I didn't want to go there, the craving for the red stuff was manageable at the moment. So instead, I wiped my hand against my jeans. Just like I had with my wings and claws, I thought about them not being there, and they withdrew back into my gums. To be honest, it felt like having a tooth pulled out, but in reverse.

Feeling and looking like the Kiera I had grown to know over the last twenty years, I thrust my hands into my coat pockets, bent my head against the snow, and headed across the featureless moors. How far away from the truck I was, I didn't know. I had been flying, not for too long, but at a great speed, so I couldn't be sure of the distance I had travelled in pursuit of Hunt and Munn.

The walk gave me time to think but not make a plan as such. How could I plan for anything anymore? I was meant to be heading to The Hollows with the others. In his letter, Ravenwood said that I should seek out someone by the name of Coanda who lived in The Hollows. How was he going to help me? And what of this choice I had to make? Did I really have to decide which race would survive? Would it be the humans or the Vampyrus? How could I ever make a decision like that? I was half human and half Vampyrus – how could I choose between them? Potter had said the whole thing was just a fairy tale, something of myth and legend. To him, Elias Munn was no more real than Father Christmas.

But what of Potter? In my heart, I could feel the nagging doubts that were growing there. When I thought of him, all I could see was him striding across the floor of the facility and driving his fist into Eloisa's chest, tearing out her heart in one quick, sudden movement. Why had he done that? I know Potter could be cranky at times and he had a temper, but that was so out of character for him. Don't get me wrong, I wasn't Eloisa's biggest fan but hey, did she really need to be murdered like that just so Potter could avenge Murphy's death? It scared me to think Potter could be capable of doing something like that. I couldn't help but remember what Ravenwood had written to me in his letter.

"..Elias Munn plunged his fist into her chest and tore her heart out..."

Those words kept going over and over in my mind since I'd seen Potter tear Eloisa's heart from her chest. But there were also other parts of that letter that just wouldn't go away. They kept flashing across my mind like giant, neon words.

"But be careful, Kiera, of who you befriend and love on your journey, for it is said that if Elias Munn can get the half-breed to love him, as a father, or a brother, or a lover, then just like his first love – he would have taken your heart as his own and he will be given the power to choose which race lives and which race dies."

Reading those words again in my mind's eye, my heart sank as I thought of Potter and I prayed that he wasn't the invisible man, Elias Munn. How could he be? Had he really just snatched Hunt from beneath my nose and killed him? Potter had gone back to the zoo to rescue Luke; he was miles away from here. Pulling the collar of my coat tight about my neck, I moved on and I hoped more than anything that my growing suspicions for Potter were wrong, because I had fallen in love with him.

Chapter Three

In the distance I could see a coil of smoke bellowing up into the night sky. I headed towards it but kept as low as possible, darting between rocks and the odd outcrop of trees. Just like I had with my wings, claws, and fangs, I looked at an object in the distance, and at a blink of an eye, I was there. When that happened, everything around me almost seemed to speed up, blur out of focus – out of time. But there was something else. It made me feel as if I was being stretched in some way, dragged towards the object that I wanted to be near. I'd felt it before, back at the police station in the town of Wasp Water as I'd sped across the canteen towards Jack Seth.

I had seen the others, Potter, Luke, and Murphy flit from one place to another in what looked like a spray of shadows, and I wondered if that's what I looked like now, fluttering from place to place in a blink of an eye. Now this was one Vampyrus trait that I didn't mind having, I smiled to myself.

Appearing behind a cluster of jagged rocks, I peered over them. The smoke was coming from the truck, which lay on its side in the snow. From my hiding place I could see the tear in the roof where Hunt had been yanked through. There were two figures by the truck and I peered through the darkness at them. My heart leapt with joy at the sight of Kayla and Isidor. Standing, I left my hiding place and ran towards them. Upon seeing me, Kayla threw open her arms and hugged me.

"We thought they had taken you," Kayla said.

"No," I told her, shaking my head. "Elias Munn got away."

"So he was in the truck then?" Isidor asked, pulling a stake from the dead Vampyrus who had been driving the truck. Seeing me looking at him, he shrugged and said, "I can't afford to waste any. I haven't got many stakes left."

"He wasn't in the truck," I told them.

"But you said he got away," Kayla said, looking confused.

I looked at her, then at Isidor. Should I tell them that their father was in the back of that truck, used as a decoy, only to be murdered by the real Elias Munn? What good would it do?

Hadn't Kayla and Isidor come to believe that their father was already dead? It would do no good to tell them he had been alive after all but only now had he been murdered. Potter had managed to turn them both around. He hadn't done it in a way I would have chosen, but it had worked. They had both stopped focusing on their grief and were now focused on the journey that lay ahead of us. Perhaps Potter had been right; they could do all their grieving after this was over. If they were to survive what lay ahead, they needed to be strong both physically and mentally. By telling them now that I had just buried their father, a few miles from here beneath a pile of broken branches and leaves, would only set them back. But if I were being truly honest with myself, I just didn't have the heart to tell Kayla. I just couldn't do it to her.

So rightly or wrongly, I guessed I might never know, I pulled them both close and said, "It was just a Vampyrus they used as a decoy so the real Elias Munn could escape."

"Where is this Vampyrus now?" Isidor asked, raising his crossbow.

"He's dead," I told them and that wasn't a lie, but what I said next was. "I killed him."

"Good," Kayla said, looking at me. "The more Vampyrus and vampire we kill, the better."

"I don't know if that's the answer," I said. I looked at Kayla and could see the anger and hurt in her eyes and knew then that I had made the right decision in not telling her about her father. So changing the subject, I asked, "What happened to my mum and Phillips? You went after them, right?"

"Just like Munn, they got away," Isidor explained. Then looking up at the sky with its snow-filled clouds he added, "This storm doesn't help. I lost Phillips in some low-flying cloud."

"Your mum had too much of a head start on me," Kayla said. "I lost sight of her."

"Maybe it was for the best," I told them.

"How come?" Kayla asked me.

"What would you have done even if you had caught up with her and Philips?" I asked.

"Ripped her throat out," Kayla said matter-of-factly.

"That's my mum you're talking about," I half-smiled. I couldn't be angry with Kayla for what she just said. But somewhere deep inside, I still clung to the hope that I could save my mum.

"She isn't your mum anymore, Kiera," Isidor cut in. "She's like the rest of them now. Lost to the red stuff."

"But we've managed to overcome it," I said. "Perhaps she could too."

Kayla looked at me and her eyes seemed full of sorrow as she said, "Kiera, don't bank on it."

"Why?" I asked.

Kayla nodded in the direction of the drivers cab.

I turned towards the truck and could see one of the Vampyrus hanging half in and half out of the shattered windscreen. I couldn't tell what sex or even how old it had been as its face was missing. White lumps of skull and cheekbone glistened wetly through what was left of the flesh.

Turning away, I faced Kayla and asked, "Did you do that?"

Nodding, Kayla said, "It wasn't intentional at first. Once I'd lost sight of your mum, I raced back after the truck to help you. I smashed through the windscreen and pulled the two Vampyrus out. They fought with me, but I was quickly joined by Isidor. The Vampyrus bit and clawed at me, so I bit back. At first, I just ripped off its nose and ears, but the blood tasted good and I just lost it, you know, went kind of crazy. Before I knew what was happening, Isidor was yanking me off the Vampyrus. It was then that I realised I had eaten his face clean off."

"Kayla, you can't carry on like this!" I barked at her, but as soon as the words were out, I regretted the tone I had used.

Kayla flinched backwards and her eyes glowed momentarily. "I'm sorry," she hissed. "But we can't all be like you, Kiera and have total control."

"I didn't mean to shout at you," I told her, knocking snow from my hair. "It's just that you were right about my

16

mum; she is lost to the red stuff and lost to me. I just don't want that to happen to you, Kayla."

"Why not?" She snapped, still hurting from how I had spoken to her. I squeezed her shoulder and said, "Because you're like a sister, Kayla." Then looking at Isidor I added, "I love both of you as if you were my family. You are my family now."

Kayla and Isidor looked at me through the falling snow, but before either of them had a chance to say anything, someone from behind us spoke, saying, "What about me? Can you find it in your heart to love me, Kiera Hudson?"

Chapter Four

Together we looked back and saw Jack Seth standing in the shadows. His tall skeletal frame loomed up into the darkness, and if he had been any taller, it seemed like his head would disappear into the clouds. Snow covered the baseball cap he had fixed on his head and his yellow eyes blazed from within his sunken eye sockets. His denim shirt was open at the throat and the red bandana he had tied about his neck fluttered in the wind. One of his hands swung loosely by his sides and the other was hidden behind his back. The hand I could see was covered in what looked like black tar, but when I stared harder, I could see that his fingers were streaked with blood.

The last time I saw him, he had gone bounding away after Sparky as he'd fled the truck in the shape of a wolf.

"Well, Kiera Hudson, can you find it in your heart to love me?" he smiled, and his lips cut a crooked line across his emaciated face.

"Why should I love you?" I asked him, the thought repulsing me.

"How about you?" he asked, looking at Kayla. Then, glancing at Isidor he added, "And what about you?"

"Why should any of us love you?" Kayla snapped, taking a step forward.

"I've just caught your mother's killer," he smiled at Kayla. Then, yanking on something, Sparky appeared from the shadows. He fell before us, a length of rope tied about his neck, the other fixed in Seth's bony hand.

Sparky made a whiny noise in the back of his throat. He looked up at us and I could see that his face was flushed red with a spattering of painful-looking boils. His glasses lay crooked across the bridge of his nose, and the right lens looked frosted with ice where it had been cracked. His black hair hung across his forehead, and his clothes were spattered with blood. I could see a huge bite mark down the length of his left thigh and his jeans were torn and coloured black with blood. Then, as if a bright light had been turned on inside my skull, I could see Seth racing after him, his heart thumping with revenge for the death of his son, Nik. When Sparky had been within his reach, Seth had lunged forward. I looked at Sparky's wounded leg again and could see where Seth had ripped away most of his thigh.

Not taking his eyes off mine, Sparky tried to stand, but he fell again and screamed out in pain. He covered the bite mark with his hands, and I watched as streams of black blood oozed through his fingers. Smiling to himself, Seth pulled on the noose and Sparky rolled over, his screams cutting through the night.

"Enough already!" I hissed at Seth.

"Enough?" Kayla questioned me as if lost and bewildered. "How can that be enough after everything that he's done? He killed my mum!"

"I know he did," I said, not able to take my eyes off the pitiful creature that now rolled around in the snow at my feet. "We've all got good enough reasons to want him dead, but we're better than him."

"Are we?" Isidor asked, raising his bow and aiming at Sparky's upturned face. "He killed my auntie, the woman I believed was my mother for all those years. She was the woman who loved me and brought me up when my father gave me away."

"And if it wasn't for scum like this, my son Nik would still be alive," Seth said as he ground the heel of his boot into Sparky's open wound.

Sparky's cries were ear-shattering as he twisted and contorted on the ground beneath the heel of Seth's boot. His eyes bulged from his head and his tongue lolled from the corner of his mouth as he screamed over and over again. Racing forward, I shoved Seth in the chest with my hands and sent him flying backwards.

"I said enough!" I shouted over Sparky's screams.

"Why are you protecting him?" Kayla asked, rushing forward.

"Because we don't just kill him," I told her. "We're not God, none of us are. He should be given the opportunity of a trial."

"A trial by whom?" Seth sneered as he came back towards me.

"The elders," I snapped back. "They tried you for the murders of those women."

"And what a lot of good they were," Seth barked. "They convicted an innocent man!"

"You wanted them to convict you!" I snapped back. "You wanted to take the blame for your son. If they'd known the true facts of the case, it would have been Nik who had gone to prison – not you!"

"So what you're saying, Kiera, is that we take him back to The Hollows with us and hand him over to the elders?" Isidor asked, still aiming his crossbow at Sparky.

"Yes," I replied.

"You're wrong, Kiera," Kayla hissed. "He can't be trusted. He'll trick us, deceive us, and kill us as we sleep."

"No..." a feeble voice murmured and we all looked down to see that it was Sparky who had spoken. With one blood-stained hand, he reached up to us, his face a mask of pain and fear. "Please don't kill me...show me some mercy."

"Like the mercy you showed my mother!" Kayla roared, and before I had the chance to stop her, she sprung forward and was tightening the rope about Sparky's throat. His eyes bulged again and he clawed at the noose with his fingers, trying to wedge them between his neck and the rope.

"Kayla!" I shouted. "Stop it!"

"No, Kiera!" she roared back. "He killed my mum, he murdered those half-breed children in their beds back at the Manor, he killed Murphy's daughters, and was partly responsible for his death. And he killed Isidor's auntie – he deserves to die!"

Kayla yanked on the rope, and springing forward, I brushed her away, not too hard; just enough for her to lose her balance and release the rope. Seeing the discontentment growing between me and my friends, Seth chuckled.

I looked at him and said for the benefit of everyone, "We're not cold-bloodied killers, we're better than that. I understand all of your reasons for wanting Sparky dead, I have enough of my own, but if we kill him, we become him."

"And how do you figure that?" Isidor said, crossbow still aimed at Sparky.

"Because Sparky kills in cold blood. He shows his victims no mercy. He kills out of hatred and fear," I told them. "You kill him now and you'll be doing it for all the same reasons. You'll be a mindless killer just like him," then glancing at Seth, I added, "and him."

Seth smiled at me, his black, broken teeth festering in his shrunken gums. Looking back at Kayla and Isidor, I said, "Do you really want to turn out like Seth and Sparky? Is that what you really want? Because if it is, I won't stop you," Then, releasing the rope, I walked away, giving Kayla and Isidor enough time and room to attack Sparky who still lay on the ground whimpering like a baby.

I looked back at them and saw Kayla step towards him, her claws out and raised up before her. Isidor stood as if frozen to the spot, then slowly, he lowered his crossbow and aimed it not at Sparky but at the ground. Sparky looked up and could see Kayla coming towards him, her long, black fingernails and fangs gleaming in the dark.

"Please," Sparky cried out, lacing his fingers before him as if he were about to say his prayers. "Don't kill me. I can help you."

As if deaf to his pleas, Kayla continued forward, and when just inches from him, she dived forward and snatched up the rope.

"No!" Sparky begged.

"Oh quit complaining," Kayla snapped at him. "I'm not going to kill you – not yet anyhow. But if we're to take you with us into The Hollows, then you're staying on the end of this rope where I can see you. But I promise you this, if for just one second I think you are going to harm me or my friends then I will take your head off in a heartbeat. Do you understand?"

Sparky looked at her, nodded and licked his lips.

"I said, do you understand?" she roared into his face, her claws just inches from his throat.

"Yes! Yes!" Sparky screeched and cowered back as far away from her as his leash would allow him.

Yanking on the rope, Kayla pulled him back close to her. "Don't screw around, Sparky. I promise you, I'm not that scared little girl anymore. I couldn't give a shit if you died, and in fact I hope and pray that you do break your promise, because that's all the reason I'll need to rip your fucking lungs out."

"I won't, I promise," he snivelled. Then looking at me, he added, "Thank you, Kiera."

Without saying anything, I looked away in disgust. I wasn't helping him, I was helping Kayla and Isidor to not become like him. Seth then strode forward, and grinding the heel of his boot into Sparky's open wound again, he shouted over the screams of pain, "The martyr might have saved you for now, but watch your back. You're a disgrace to the Lycanthrope."

"We're no different, Seth," Sparky wailed. "You're a killer just like me."

Ignoring him, Seth said, "You said you could help us. How?"

"I didn't say that," Sparky cried out as Seth drove down harder with his foot.

"Yeah, you did," Kayla cut in.

"What do you know?" Isidor asked.

"Nothing!" Sparky sobbed in pain.

Going to him, I pushed Seth aside, and Sparky cradled his wounded leg. "It hurts doesn't it?" I said looking down at him. "Remember how you treated me back in the zoo when my leg was wounded?"

"That wasn't me," he said, staring up at me. "It was Phillips."

"You licked my goddamn leg, you animal!" I hissed at him. "You threw me around the room and hosed me down with freezing cold water."

"It was Phillips," Sparky groaned.

Hunkering down, I looked in to his bloodshot eyes and whispered, "Sparky, this lot only needs one little excuse to rip you in half. I can only hold them off for so long. So tell me what you know."

"I don't know anything!" he cried.

"Liar," I hissed and punched his wounded leg.

Sparky's leg jerked and went rigid and I could see the pain in his eyes. They seemed to spin in their sockets. "Tell me, Sparky."

"I don't..." he started, but I hit him again, this time harder.

"Okay!" he screeched, phlegm spraying from his lips as he gripped his leg. "I know where you can find this invisible man, Elias Munn!"

"Who is he?" I demanded my heart racing.

"I didn't say I knew who he was," Sparky wailed in pain. "I said I know where he is heading – where you can find him."

"Where?" I breathed, feeling nervous at the thought that I might actually be able to catch this man once and for all.

"The Hollows," Sparky said, through gritted teeth.

"We already know that," I told him, hoping for his sake that he wasn't messing with me.

"But you don't know where in The Hollows," Sparky grimaced.

"Where?" I shouted, raising my hand as if to strike his wounded leg again.

"The Dust Palace!" Sparky whispered as if giving away a deadly secret.

"Impossible," someone said from behind us.

I spun round to see Potter standing beneath the shadows of a solitary tree that stood some feet away. Beside him stood someone else. Peering through the gloom, my heart lept at the sight of Luke. Potter had rescued him.

Standing slowly, I watched as both of them walked out from beneath the low-hanging branches of the tree and came towards me. As usual, a cigarette dangled from the corner of Potter's mouth, the blue smoke trailing away into the night. He looked at me, but it was more than looking at me; it was like he was searching my eyes, looking into me.

I broke his stare and turned towards Luke. He came towards me. His jet-black hair was longer than I remembered and hung around his shoulders. The lower half of his face was covered in a scruffy-looking beard, but this only accentuated his brilliant green eyes. His rugged good looks were still visible from beneath his beard, and although he looked as if he had lost some weight, the dirty shirt he wore still showed off his muscular chest and arms.

Luke stopped just a few inches away and looked at me. His eyes seemed to glimmer. I glanced over at Potter who had his eyes fixed on me. I quickly looked away and back at Luke. I remembered the last time that I had seen him – being kicked and beaten before me as my mother offered me a fist full of the red stuff. I had eaten it to save his life. There was an uncomfortable silence, not just between Luke and me, but throughout all of us. No one said a word and I knew without even turning to face them, they were all watching me.

My heart raced in my chest like a trip hammer and those feelings that I had felt so passionately when with Luke came rushing back. But it was more than that. The feelings which were making my heart race were not of lust or desire, but guilt and betrayal. While Luke had been suffering at the hands of Phillips, Sparky, my mother, and God knows who else, I had been making love to his friend – I had fallen in love with his best friend.

Every part of me wanted to look at Potter again, but I just couldn't. I didn't want to look into his eyes. What would I see there? So, very slowly, I walked towards Luke and hugged him.

Brushing his bristly cheek against mine, Luke whispered in my ear and said, "I never thought I would see you again, Kiera."

"I didn't think I would ever see you again either," I told him as he held me tight. I could feel his body against mine, and just as I had remembered it, it felt as hard as stone.

"What did they do to you?" I whispered, still not able to look into his face.

"It wasn't so bad," he said. "Potter told me that they hurt you, Kiera. I'm so sorry I wasn't there for you. I'll never be able to thank Potter enough for taking care of you for me."

To hear those words threw images of me and Potter across my mind, our bodies entwined as we had made love. I pushed the pictures away. Opening my eyes, I looked over

Luke's shoulder as I hugged him and could see Potter watching me. His face looked hard and haggard. But it was his eyes, there was a sadness to them – something I had only ever seen once before, the day Murphy had been murdered.

Taking the cigarette from the corner of his mouth, he flicked it away. He looked away from me, crossed to where Sparky lay nursing his leg on the ground, and kicked him in the guts. Sparky howled in agony and screwed himself into a ball.

Pulling away from Luke, I turned to face Potter and said, "What in the hell was that for?"

"He's a fucking liar!" Potter said, looking at Sparky and not at me.

"What are you talking about?" I said, heading back towards Sparky and the others as Luke followed me.

"He said that you would find this Elias Munn in the Dust Palace," Potter hissed, still unable to look at me.

"So?" I shrugged.

"That's impossible," Potter barked, and this time he did look at me. The sadness had gone from his face and was now replaced with anger.

"Why is it impossible?" Isidor asked, coming forward, his eyebrow piercing twinkling in the moonlight.

Potter looked at him, but said nothing. Instead, he shoved another cigarette into the corner of his mouth and lit it.

"Potter's right," Luke cut in. "The Dust Palace is the home of the elders. He couldn't possibly be there."

"Why not?" Kayla asked, as she brushed snow from her red hair.

Blowing smoke from his nostrils in two thin jets, Potter looked at Kayla and said, "Listen, sweetheart, you don't just stroll into the Dust Palace. It's the most sacred place in The Hollows. It's where the Elders, or as some like to call them, the gods live. It's their home. To me, I think it's just a bunch of bullshit, but one thing I do know for certain is that place is a fortress and there's only one way in."

"And where's that?" Seth asked.

"Shit, who invited you along?" Luke suddenly groaned, as if noticing Seth for the first time.

"Good to see you too, Luke Bishop," Seth snarled. "It was Potter's idea."

"I had no choice," Potter said, looking at Luke.

"Didn't you say this scum was responsible for helping to kill Murphy?" Luke asked in disbelief.

"That's right," Potter said, flicking ash from the tip of his cigarette. "But I've gone some way in getting even," he added, then glanced at me.

"How could you ever possibly get even over the death of Murphy?" Luke asked, his black beard now turning white with snow.

"Just like Seth helped take Murphy's heart, I took the heart of his lover," Potter told him, and again he looked at me, as if trying to gauge my reaction.

Those images of Potter striding across the floor of the facility and ripping Eloisa's heart out swam in front of my mind again and they sickened me. I broke Potter's gaze and looked away. I still couldn't understand why he had done that, he had confused and scared me.

"I think you'll find that I've lost more than Eloisa," Seth barked at Potter, his eyes blazing like hot coals. "I've lost my son, Nik too."

"What, you mean he's dead?" Potter asked, and for a moment I thought I could see the briefest of smirks tugging at the corner of his mouth.

"Yes," Seth spat. "He was killed in a vampire attack a few miles from here."

"Aww," Potter groaned. "My heart bleeds for you. Don't tell me anymore or I think I might just start crying."

Before anyone knew what was happening, Seth launched himself at Potter and had him by the throat. "We have unfinished business, Potter, so I wouldn't be too cocky if I were you!"

Tearing Seth's claw from his throat, Potter stared into Seth's eyes, blowing smoke into his face. "Bring it on anytime, wolf-man, I'll be ready for you."

"Oh, please." I groaned. "What is it with you two and all this schoolyard crap? Okay, so some of us don't like each other much – and that's putting it mildly – but we have to find a way of getting along, because if we can't, then we might as well die, right here, right now, and save Elias Munn the job of killing us."

"She's right you know," Luke said, stepping between Potter and Seth, pushing them apart.

Potter scowled at Seth and wandered away back towards the tree.

"So what's the one and only way into this Dust Palace?" I called after Potter.

"You have to be invited in by the gods," he shouted back over his shoulder at me. "And somehow, I can't imagine them ever inviting Elias Munn around for tea!"

"It's true, I tell you," Sparky snivelled, still clutching his stomach where Potter had kicked him.

Kneeling down beside him, I looked into his wild yellow eyes and said, "You better not be leading us into some trap!"

"I'm not, I promise," he said.

"Your promise had better be as good as mine," Kayla told him, yanking on the rope still wrapped about her fist, "or you'll be dead."

"I'm dead anyway," Sparky yelped as Kayla pulled him to his feet. "When Elias Munn discovers that I've betrayed him, he'll kill me anyway."

"Then you better start praying that we kill him first," Isidor said, placing his crossbow across his back. Then, looking at me he added, "So what's the plan, Kiera?"

Looking up into the sky, the clouds had started to spread out and the storm started to ease. It was still bitterly cold and we were all covered in a coating of snow. "We head down into The Hollows," I said, looking at Luke then over my shoulder at Potter, who was leaning against the tree with his arms folded across his chest. "I've got to find someone called Felix Coanda."

"There's no entrance to The Hollows for miles," Potter said. "And we know the whole area has been sealed off."

"What about the huge hole the Vampyrus have the humans digging?" Kayla asked.

"What hole?" Luke asked.

"We came across this...crater, I guess you could call it," I started to explain. "The Vampyrus are building some kind of giant escape hatch so they can flood the country at great speed. They've got the townsfolk from Wasp Water digging it, human slaves. It's a few miles from here."

"We could enter The Hollows from there," Luke suggested, rubbing his beard with his fingers.

"Good luck," Seth growled.

"What's that supposed to mean?" Luke asked him.

"We barely got out of there alive," Seth said. "The whole area is teaming with vampires."

"There is another way into The Hollows," Sparky said, looking at me, half-smiling.

"Where?" I snapped at him. I didn't want him to smile at me, I didn't like or trust him.

"The Vampyrus built another tunnel, an escape route if you like," he said, "just in case the main tunnel collapsed and they needed to get out."

"How can we trust you?" Luke asked him.

"We can trust him on that," I said thoughtfully.

"Why?" Luke asked.

"Remember that disc I took from the monastery?" I asked him. "Well, I had a chance to check it out on a computer back in Wasp Water and there were plans and drawings of places that the Vampyrus were using. There was a plan of what I now suspect was that huge hole they're digging. There was a tunnel leading from it, but it didn't show where it led to."

Looking at me, then at Sparky who now hobbled on one leg next to Kayla, Luke said, "Okay then, lead the way, but this better not be some kinda trick or..."

"I know, I know," Sparky whined, "or I'm dead."

Turning, Sparky limped away, Kayla only feet behind him as she held onto his leash. "This way," he said back over his shoulder. Silently, Seth and Isidor followed.

Luke took my arm and said, "Stick close to me, Kiera, I'm still not convinced we can trust Sparky." He led me away towards the mountains in the distance, and looking back over my shoulder, I could see Potter standing alone by the tree.

Chapter Five

We followed Sparky as he limped and hobbled over the rocky ground that spread out before us like a white blanket. The snow had eased, and a grey sun was just starting to peek over the horizon. It was cold and my hands felt numb, even though I had them tucked into my coat pockets.

Every so often, Kayla would pull on Sparky's leash and tell him to hurry up. How much of this she did out of spite and hatred for Sparky, or just because she was desperate to get out of the cold, I didn't know. Kayla seemed tougher now – *harder* – and I wasn't sure I liked it. But could I put the blame for the change in her solely at the feet of Potter? Yeah, he told her she needed to toughen up and prepare herself for what might lay ahead, but I wondered too if everything she had been through hadn't also changed her.

Luke walked beside me and said very little. When I did sneak a sideways glance at him, he looked lost in thought. I found it hard to strike up a conversation with him as it felt uncomfortable. I felt bad about what had happened between Potter and me while he hadn't been around. I didn't regret what had happened between us, and I wouldn't go back and change that for anything as I had fallen in love with Potter and I knew that now – but I had to tell Luke somehow and I didn't know when. The guy had just come back from hell, he had put his life on the line for me as I had for him, back in the caves beneath the Fountain of Souls. So how would he take the news that I had fallen for his best friend? What would that do to him? What would that do to the friendship between the three of us?

And what of Potter? Had I fallen for the wrong guy? However much I tried, I couldn't get those images of him ripping out Eloisa's heart out of my head. Why had he done that? And those words written by Ravenwood, "...*Elias Munn plunged his fist into her chest and tore her heart out...*"

Had Potter really murdered Sophie in that way? Had he slipped up in front of me by killing Eloisa in the same manner? The only way I would know for sure was to ask him. Looking back over my shoulder, I could just make out his lonely figure as he followed us up the mountainside from some distance away. Slowing down, I decided to hang back and wait for him so we could talk.

Noticing that I was no longer beside him, Luke said, "Hey Kiera, we don't have much time to lose, keep up."

"What about Potter?" I asked.

"He's big and ugly enough to look after himself," Luke smiled at me.

"All the same, I still think we should..." I started.

Then, blowing warm breath over his hands, Luke said, "C'mon, Kiera, it's freezing out here." Taking my arm, he pulled me close to him. Gently, I pushed his hand away.

"Is everything okay?" Luke asked, a look of puzzlement on his face.

"Everything's fine," I said, starting to move forward again.

"Are you sure?" Luke asked, catching up with me.

"It's just that I don't need to be told what to do, okay?" I told him. "I've survived this long. Things have changed, Luke. I've changed."

"What do you mean?" he asked, sounding surprised.

"Look, all I'm saying is that I've had to learn to fend for myself over the last few months," I explained. "So it's hard for me to have you tell me what to do and what's best for me."

"I wasn't trying to tell you what to do, Kiera," he said softly. "I just didn't want you to get cold."

"I'm already cold," I half-smiled.

"Okay, I'm sorry," he said. "It's just...it's just that I still care for you, Kiera. My feelings for you haven't changed. I still lov-"

"Please, Luke," I said, looking away from him. "Don't say any more."

"Okay, I won't for now" he whispered, and we walked the rest of the way in silence.

Halfway up the mountainside, Sparky turned down a narrow crevice set between two giant slabs of granite stone. The wind whistled through the gap and sounded like the cries of lost children searching for their mums. This break between the mountains was only wide enough for us to walk single file and Sparky led the way, shuffling onwards and mumbling in pain. Looking at him like that made me remember how he had once been. He had been my friend, or so I thought. We had shared coffee together at Starbucks, gone to see movies, sat in front of the T.V. in my poky flat back in Havensfield while we ate my poor attempts at cooking. That was when we had been friends, and all the while, little did I know he was watching me, keeping an eye on me, until Elias Munn was ready to strike.

I could feel little pity for him, as he had brought this situation upon himself. But still, it was hard for me to reconcile what he had once been and what he had now become. I could see fear in his eyes. I had seen it back at the truck and it hadn't been fear of being killed by any of us – his fear was of Munn.

We made our way through the narrow fissure in the rock, which led out to a narrow ledge running around the side of the mountain. Sparky sniffed the air, looked back at us and said, "This way."

The path was narrow and one slip would have sent any one of us crashing down the side of the mountain. Low-flying cloud swept past and gave me the sense of being in another world. The mountain stretched up high above us, and below in the distance, I could just make out the huge crater that the Vampyrus had the humans digging. Vehicles filled with rock they had removed still came and went. Peeking through the cloud, the crater looked huge, like a giant mouth in the earth which was soon to spew hundreds or thousands of Vampyrus above ground to take to the skies and attack villages, towns, and cities across the country. I couldn't help but remember the nightmare I had while staying at Hallowed Manor. I'd dreamt of London being overridden by the Vampyrus. Black-winged creatures had flown through the sky, so many of them that they had blocked out the sun. St Paul's Cathedral had been reduced to rubble; Big Ben had been burning like a giant candle; vampires had rampaged through the streets feeding on any surviving humans. Had that been just a nightmare? Knowing now what the Vampyrus had planned, I knew that it was a premonition of what was to come. Why was I now so certain? I'd also dreamt of the London underground being overrun with Vampyrus and vampires and that had happened. Watching the T.V. back at Kenner's Farm as we had fled those vampire-cops, I had seen the news reports claiming that wild animals had gone berserk down below ground.

Knowing what was going to come didn't help. Perhaps it should have – I mean, who wouldn't want to know what their enemy had planned for them in the future? Any army would want to know that. But the task ahead seemed too much. There were only a handful of us against thousands upon thousands of bloodthirsty Vampyrus. Knowing that didn't inspire me – it scared me. And like the mountain we now climbed, the end of our journey appeared to be too far out of reach for me to be confident in an outcome that would save the human race. But whichever way I looked at it, the humans or the Vampyrus had to die and I had to decide that. However hard I thought of a way out of it, I couldn't see one.

Just say what Ravenwood had written in his letter was true. What if I did have to choose between the human race and the Vampyrus – how could I ever make such a decision? How could I let an entire species die? How would I decide? Spin a coin?

"I do not have to tell you that the burden on you is a great one. The fate of two entire races lies in your hands. The decision to destroy an entire race is not an easy one – so choose wisely, Kiera Hudson." The words that Ravenwood had scrawled inside that book kept flashing across my mind and I wanted to scream out at them – tear them up, set fire to them. But I'd already done that and even as I'd watched those words disappear in a ball of flames, I knew in my heart they wouldn't really go. They would be burnt into my mind until I made that terrible decision, and with every step I took around the mountainside, that decision was getting nearer and nearer.

Then, as if speaking in the wind that whipped about me, Ravenwood's voice whispered in my ear the passage from his letter that had haunted me since I'd read it.

"But be careful, Kiera, of who you befriend and love on

your journey, for it is said that if Elias Munn can get the half-breed to love him as a father, or a brother, or a lover, then just like his first love – he would have taken your heart as his own and he will be given the power to choose which race lives and which race dies."

Without being able to help myself, I glanced back over my shoulder and could see Potter making his way around the ledge some way behind us. His head was down as if in deep thought or prayer. But, knowing Potter, he wouldn't be praying. There was something on his mind and it was more than just his fear that I might truly be in love with his best friend Luke. No, there was something else. If Potter really was Elias Munn, I knew that I'd fallen in love with him, and although that scared me, there was little voice inside me that said, *"Kiera, pass the decision to him. Let him choose which race survives. It wouldn't be your fault; no one can truly help who they fall in love with..."*

"No!" I hissed to myself. "That's the coward's way out!"

"What?" Luke suddenly said, looking back at me.

"What?" I said.

"You said something," he smiled, looking bemused.

"Did I?"

"It sounded like you did."

"Must have been the wind," I smiled and glanced back again at Potter. This time he wasn't looking down, but directly at me. I looked away.

Ahead, Sparky slowed, then came to a stop. The path had come to a sudden end and it led to a sheer drop down into the crater below.

"Is this some sort of a joke?" Seth asked, peering from beneath his snow-covered baseball cap.

"He's tricked us," Kayla spat, and yanked hard on Sparky's leash.

"No, no," Sparky winced as his head snapped forward as the noose was pulled by Kayla. "Look over there."

We all looked in the direction Sparky was now pointing. Opposite was another mountain, and carved into the side of it was a doorway. It looked odd and out of place, a nondescript-looking wooden door set into the side of a mountain with no path, steps, or ladder leading to it.

"That leads down into The Hollows and that crater. See, I didn't let you down. Not this time, Kiera," he said staring at me with a pitiful look in his eyes.

"How do we get over to it?" Isidor asked, looking over at the door.

"What do you think God gave you wings for?" someone cut in, and we all looked back to see Potter had caught up with us.

"But I can't," Seth said, scowling at Potter.

"Not my problem, Seth," Potter snapped. "Perhaps you should go back down the mountain and ask the good vampires down at that hole if they'll let you in the front door."

Ignoring Potter, Seth looked at Luke somewhat embarrassed, and said, "Would you carry me?"

"Why do you want to come with us anyway?" Luke asked back. "This is as far as you come. I'm not taking a Lycanthrope down into The Hollows."

"Not unless I'm in handcuffs, eh?" Seth barked. "You didn't mind dragging me down there when you thought you had captured your killer."

"Oh, change your tune for fuck's sake," Potter groaned. "You're getting on my tits now. You're a killer, your entire race is nothing more than a bunch of mindless killers. You may not have killed those women – you now say it was your son – but you've killed plenty in your time. Now, do us all a favour and piss off back to those caves beneath the fountain of trolls or whatever it is you call it."

"Souls!" Seth barked.

"Whatever," Potter growled back.

"I'm sorry, Seth..." Luke started.

"Don't be sorry, Luke, for crying out loud," Potter shouted. "He led us into a trap back at that lake and that's what got Murphy killed. When are you going to stop putting your trust in this scum? We've just followed the pizza-boy halfway up a mountain to some doorway set into a mountainside, and we don't know what's on the other side of that door!"

"Pizza-boy?" Sparky whimpered.

"I think he's talking about those spots on your face," Isidor said. "Get used to it, he says that sort of shit to me all the time."

"I've told you the truth," Sparky howled at Potter.

"Truth?" Potter stammered in disbelief. "Your kind wouldn't know what the truth was if your pathetic little lives depended on it." Then turning to Kayla, he added, "Cut the mutt loose, we go on without the werewolves."

"You can't do this," Seth barked. "I have the right to get revenge for the death of my son."

"What about Eloisa?" I suddenly cut in, looking at Seth then quickly at Potter.

"What?" Seth said.

"Well Potter ripped her heart out. Don't you want to avenge her death?" I asked him.

"I've many lovers, Kiera Hudson," Seth half-smiled at me, his eyes glowing. "She was okay, but let's just say I don't like my lovers to be so willing – I like a woman who will offer some resistance – you know, play the victim."

Looking into his crazy spinning eyes, I said, "You really are an animal, aren't you?"

"Jeez, at last the penny has dropped!" Potter sighed. "What do you think I've been trying to tell you?"

Turning to face Potter, I said, "And you're no better. You ripped her heart out just so you could get back at Seth – and he doesn't even give a crap."

Hearing my words, Potter almost seemed to flinch as if I'd slapped him hard across the face. He looked as if he wanted to say something, but before he had the chance, I'd turned my back to him to find Seth ripping the skin from his own face.

It fell away in fleshy strips and his snout sprung out, white foamy saliva spraying from his jaws.

"If I don't go," he snarled, "None of us go!" Pulling his chest apart, revealing a mass of bristling black fur, he rolled his head back and began to howl.

Chapter Six

Seth's deep booming roar reverberated off the mountainsides like thunder. The whole mountain shook, sending rocks spilling down onto us from high above. The breath from his giant mouth was hot and blew my hair off my face.

Looking over the edge of the cliff, I could see the vehicles below stop; in fact, everything stopped as the vampires and Vampyrus below looked up to investigate. Within moments, there was an ear-splitting squawking noise as the Vampyrus launched themselves into the air and came racing up the side of the mountain towards us, their wings beating so loud that it almost masked the sound of Seth's continuous roar.

Peering over my shoulder at the advancing Vampyrus, Potter said, "We've got company!"

No sooner had the words left his mouth, Jack Seth's howls became a scream as Potter disappeared from beside me, only to reappear an instant later hovering in the air. If I'd blinked, I would have missed it, but with one mighty swoop of his claw he knocked Seth from the mountainside. The wolf spun away into the air, and before it had disappeared into the cloud, it had taken human form again, and I was sure that Seth's yellow eyes were staring at me.

Sweeping around in the air, Potter watched Seth bounce helplessly against the jagged mountainside and disappear

"Now *that* was for Murphy, you piece of shit!" Potter said grimly.

Seeing one of his own die so suddenly and fearing he would be next, Sparky took the rope that was fastened to him and yanked at it. Loosing her footing, Kayla slipped on the snow-covered edge and went toppling over. She clung to the rope and Sparky cut through it with his claw.

"Luke!" Kayla screamed as she was snatched away from the side of the cliff face by one of the Vampyrus that had raced up towards us.

Tearing his crossbow from his back in a flash of movement, Isidor had released two arrows which sliced straight into the head of the Vampyrus who had his sister. Somersaulting from the edge of the cliff, Isidor was in the air snatching Kayla away from the now dead Vampyrus.

Launching himself through the air, his shirt flying away as his wings shot from his back, Luke took hold of Sparky's ears. With a quick flick of his wrists and a hideous tearing noise, Luke had torn Sparky's head in two. Lumps of brain splattered the cliff face like pools of hot, grey jelly. Sparky's body slumped onto the ledge, where it twitched and jerked uncontrollably. Swooping out of the sky, Potter kicked out at it and I watched it roll down the mountainside.

Winking back at Luke, Potter said, "Just like the good old days. There's nothing better than killing Lycanthrope!"

Smiling back at his friend, Luke agreed and said, "Just like the old days!"

Shocked at the speed and apparent heartlessness in which they had just slaughtered Seth and Sparky, I gasped and shouted, "You two are unbelievable!"

"Thanks, sweet cheeks," Potter beamed, and it was the first time I had seen him smile since returning from the zoo with Luke.

"That wasn't a compliment!" I screamed at him over the sound of the approaching Vampyrus.

Swooping past me so close that his face brushed against mine, he whispered in my ear, "I know, but secretly, you just can't get enough of it!" Then he was gone, rocketing away and biting and clawing at the Vampyrus that were rapidly filling the sky all around us.

I looked at Luke who said, "I don't know how we're going to get out of this one!" Then he too was gone, spiralling through the air so fast that all I could see was a streak of black, like after burn coming from a jet fighter.

Throwing off my coat and rolling back my shoulders, I ran towards the edge of the ledge and dived into the air.

Please let my wings open! I prayed and shut my eyes.

Instead of falling, I felt myself soaring, and it was exhilarating. I could feel the cold air rush past me at an incredible speed. Opening my eyes, I looked down and had to stop myself from screaming. I didn't know how high I'd climbed but the crater now looked like a pinprick in the earth below. Tilting slightly forward, I started to plummet downwards, but I still didn't feel confident in my ability to fly. Looking back at my wings as they rippled on either side of me, I knew it was something I would have to master quickly or I would soon be killed by the two Vampyrus who were racing after me.

Rolling to my right, I cut through the sky and the two Vampyrus sped past me. Looking back I could see them momentarily disappear into a grey mountain of cloud, then come screaming out of it towards me. Flipping around, I angled my wings backwards and dropped through the sky. The air hit my chest like I'd just crashed into a brick wall and I feared that the pressure of it would break my ribs. My cheeks rippled and I felt as if I couldn't breathe. But I knew I had to, so breathing through my nose, I felt the icy cold air sting the back of my throat. Faster and faster I raced back towards the ground, and with every second I lost altitude, I feared I would never be able to stop. How had I done it before? Had I arched my back somehow? Pushing out my chest and locking my arms tight beside me, I arched my back and at once, as if I'd stepped on an invisible set of brakes, I slowed.

The Vampyrus that were behind me rushed past, as if taken by surprise by my sudden stop. One of them had sharper reflexes and swooped away before smashing into the rocky ground below. But the other wasn't as quick, and I watched as it dive-bombed into a razor-sharp outcrop of rock. Its severed arms and legs bounced back into the air in a crimson spray of blood. Hovering, I watched as several vampires that had been forcing the humans to dig the crater, race over and begin to fight over the bloody remains of the Vampyrus.

It was then, as I raced back up into the dawn sky, that I saw the rest of the Vampyrus which had been protecting the crater soar up into the sky. As the Vampyrus raced amongst the clouds, the clouds changed colour. They were no longer reflecting the colour of the rising sun; they were turning grey, dark grey, charcoal, then black. Then suddenly, they began to separate as if falling apart into smaller pieces. These then broke up into smaller pieces, and then into black wispy fragments as the Vampyrus swarmed out of them and back towards us.

I saw Potter fly away from a Vampyrus he had just sliced the wings from, and it plummeted away through the sky. Banking, I raced towards him.

"Look! They're coming out of the clouds!" I shouted over the roar of the wind.

"There's hundreds of them!" Potter yelled back.

The Vampyrus that had swept from the clouds swarmed around in the air as if preparing to attack. Then, to my horror, they came racing towards us. And as they came, they made those hideous squawking sounds that pierced the air. Their cries of hatred and anger seemed to penetrate right through me, making my heart thunder in my chest. I could see that their bodies were black, hairy and bloated. Although they closely resembled giant vampire bats, they had bony-looking legs and a set of wings that were transparent and covered in bristly hair. Just like I had seen Luke in his true Vampyrus form at Hallowed Manor, these creatures no longer resembled human beings, but giant winged creatures. Noses turned up, long pointed ears, and jaws full of razor-like fangs.

The Vampyrus were nearly upon us and as they drew within range, Potter banked violently, rolled to the left and sharply lost altitude. I felt my stomach leap into my throat as I banked and raced after Potter. Ahead, I could see Isidor, and Potter was racing towards him.

I caught up in time to hear Potter shout at Isidor. "I'm not usually one for retreating, kid, but we'd better get out of here!"

"To where?" Isidor roared back.

Then, as if from nowhere, Luke swept up beside us and pointing back towards the mountain, he bellowed, "Look! Over there!"

Turning in the air, we stared in the direction he was pointing. The doorway we'd seen earlier was now open and a winged man hovered before it. Raising an arm in the air, he beckoned us towards him.

"Who's that?" Kayla asked as she came racing towards us.

"Felix Coanda, if I'm not mistaken," Luke said peering ahead.

"Then what are we waiting for?" I said, looking over my shoulder at the approaching Vampyrus. "Let's go!"

Curling my claws into a fist, I punched forward and soared back towards the mountain and the open doorway. Was this it? Was I really going to finally enter The Hollows?

Chapter Seven

I swept towards the door where Felix Coanda hovered in front of it. His wings were mottled-looking, like something you would find sticking out of the back of a moth. His skin, just like Potter's and Luke's, was corpse white. He had pale blue lips and a set of fangs that looked as sharp as knives. His hair was black and wiry and stuck out in thick clumps, giving him the appearance he had just crawled out of bed. His eyes shone a fierce blue and they kind of reminded me of Murphy's. He was older than Luke and Potter; I guessed about forty-years-old. He was stripped to the waist, but his upper body, although slim, was muscular. Black hair covered his chest and spread over his shoulders and down his arms, like a fine coat of fur. I had only ever seen one other Vampyrus have such a thick coating of hair even though they were in human form, and that was Ravenwood, but his hair had been snow white.

"Quick!" Coanda shouted, coaxing me forward with his giant claws. "Faster! Faster, I tell you!"

As I raced towards him, I could see that he was glancing nervously past me. Looking back, I could see Potter and the others racing behind me, followed by a mass of screaming Vampyrus. They clutched at them with their claws. Kayla streaked forward, her red hair gleaming in the morning sun, giving her the appearance of being on fire.

"Faster!" Coanda roared again, and I flipped round to see him holding the door open for us, and beyond it all I could see was darkness. A doorway hundreds of feet above the ground set in the side of a mountain, leading to a world hidden hundreds of miles beneath the Earth. Was I ready for this? I knew I had to be, as I shot through the open doorway and into a world of darkness.

The others rushed in behind me into the narrow passageway that, just like Sparky had said, had been gouged into the mountainside. Looking back over my shoulder, I saw the oblong shape of daylight disappear as Coanda slammed the door shut on the approaching Vampyrus. But almost immediately there was light again, just the faintest chinks at first. Then they grew longer and wider, as the Vampyrus on the other side of the door ripped it to pieces with their claws.

"This wasn't part of the plan!" Coanda shouted as he raced past me, his wings brushing against my face.

"What do you mean?" I called after him.

"Couldn't you lot use the front door like everybody else?" he snapped over his shoulder. "I heard you were all a bunch of mavericks, but this takes the piss!"

"You mean there's a front door?" I breathed, looking back at the one that was now being ripped to splinters by the Vampyrus who flew about outside.

"There ain't no front door, sweet cheeks," Potter answered as he flexed his claws, readying himself for the Vampyrus that were breaking their way into the tunnel. "The guy's an arsehole!"

"I didn't think you knew him?" I asked.

"Never met him," Potter snapped as he faced the door. "But I've heard he's meant to be some hotshot flying ace – all the women love him, apparently!"

"They're breaking through!" Luke roared, as the first of the Vampyrus stuck its hideous-looking snout through the gaps in the doorway.

"Then *run!*" Coanda shouted, as he made his way down the tunnel.

"Hotshot my arse," Potter growled, as he lunged at the Vampyrus' colossal head as it poked through the door, removing its eyes with his claws. The creature screamed, thrashing its head from left to right as if it had become stuck. Flicking its eyeballs from the tips of his claws, Potter looked at Luke, and grinning he said, "That should slow them down!" Then he was gone, racing away down the corridor behind Coanda.

"Go! Go! Go!" Luke urged us, and without any further hesitation, Kayla, Isidor, and I fled into The Hollows.
The tunnel spiralled downwards, deeper and deeper it went. It was dark, so dark that even I had trouble seeing through it. But ahead I could hear Coanda drawing breath as he raced

42

onwards. The others tripped and stumbled behind me, and a couple of times I had to stop and help Kayla up as she fell in the dark.

"Take my hand," I told her. Gripping it, we raced forward. Then from behind, I heard the sound of screeching and squawking, and in the confines of the tunnel the sound was deafening and terrifying. Hearing those sounds, I knew the Vampyrus had managed to break down the door and were now racing through the tunnel in pursuit of us. With my heart pounding, we raced on, faster and faster, navigating the twists and bends in the narrow tunnel. How far we had travelled down into the earth I couldn't be sure; we had raced at such speeds that I didn't know the distance we had gone. Eventually the ground began to level, and in the darkness ahead, I could see a fork in the tunnel. Racing towards it, Coanda came to a sudden stop and we all nearly clattered into him. Kayla tugged at my hand and we veered to the right.

"Not that way!" Coanda barked, his bright blue eyes gleaming in the darkness. "That way leads to the crater and thousands more of those Vampyrus."

"Which way?" Isidor gasped, the sounds of the approaching Vampyrus growing ever closer.

Looking at Luke and Potter, Coanda barked, "You two, give me a hand with this."

"With what?" Potter snapped back.

"This!" Coanda said taking hold of a giant boulder that was set against the wall which blocked the left fork of the tunnel. Together Potter, Luke, and Coanda, heaved the giant stone aside, revealing a small passageway on the other side of it. Screwing up my eyes, I could see that it was barely big enough to crawl into.

"What you waiting for, Christmas?" Coanda hissed. "Into the hole!"

Crouching on all fours, I forced my way into the hole and the others raced in behind me. Halfway down the tunnel, I could see a pinprick of light in the distance. Behind me, I could hear Coanda, Luke, and Potter dragging the boulder back over the entrance, and as they did, the sound of the approaching

Vampyrus fell silent.

    With only one way to go, I crawled forward towards that speck of light.

Chapter Eight

The white light ahead wasn't the end of the tunnel as I had first thought. It was a light of sorts, but not like any other I had seen before. It glowed - no it pulsed - a sickly yellow colour and it seemed to be coming from the walls of the tunnel ahead. As I grew closer still, I could see it was a plant that scaled the walls, lighting my way. It was thick and ropey, like illumines seaweed. It smelt too - sweet like toffee apples. I crawled further down the tunnel, the others behind me, and my hands hurt against the surface which felt as if it was covered in loose stone chippings.

Fixated on the glowing plant ahead, I failed to notice what was beneath me, and as if having all the air sucked from my lungs, I suddenly began to plummet downwards. The ground beneath me had suddenly fallen away. I dropped into utter darkness and couldn't help but scream. As I fell, I heard Kayla and Isidor cry out above me as they, too, started to fall.

Had we just been led into another trap by Coanda? Was he going to be someone else who had deceived me? With my mind scrambling, I couldn't really think about that now, and I clutched at the air for something to grab onto. But there was nothing. Then, just like a parachute opening, my wings rolled open and I began to slow. They beat frantically on either side of me and matched the rhythm of my pounding heart. Then my eyes, as they always did, began to adjust to the darkness that smothered me like a rug. I looked left and right, then up. Above me I could see Kayla and Isidor as their own wings opened and slowed their descent.

"Where are we?" Kayla called out into the darkness, her voice sounding panicked.

"I don't know!" Isidor called back, both of their voices echoed as if they were shouting into some giant well.

"Kiera, is that you? I can't see you but I can hear your heart and wings beating!" Kayla shouted.

"I can see you," I tried to reassure her. "It looks like we fell into some giant hole."

"But we're still falling!" Isidor yelled. "I can't fly back up to the surface - it's like we're being pulled down."

I knew exactly what Isidor meant. It was like the darkness was some kind of quicksand, which was sucking us further and further below ground.

"You're in a drop shaft," a voice said very close to me. I spun around in the air, Coanda was falling beside me. Then, half-smiling, he added, "There's only one way you can go and that's down."

Before I had a chance to say anything back, he was gone, flying away beneath me.

Kayla and Isidor drew level with me.

"Did he say we were in a drop shaft?" Isidor asked me.

"I think so," I told him, all the time being sucked into the darkness below.

"Wow," Isidor breathed. "I'd heard about these things as a kid, but I thought they had all been sealed up."

"Why?" Kayla asked.

"They had a tendency of collapsing..." he started.

"Just like this one!" Potter suddenly shouted as he nosedived past us and down into the blackness.

"What!" I called out, after him.

"Kiera, the drop shaft is gonna collapse!" another voice said, and by the time I realised it had been Luke who had spoken, he was gone, rocketing away beneath me.

The shaft began to vibrate, shake, then rumble. Within seconds, the sound of falling rock became deafening - it was louder than any thunder I had ever heard and I had a quick snapshot of my mum leaving the house that day in the thunder storm. Then the memory was gone and I was looking up into the shaft as it began to cave in above us. But it looked odd. It was like a solid mass of darkness racing towards us like a tidal wave.

Shoving Kayla and Isidor out of the path of a falling piece of giant rock, I screamed at them, "Go!"

Without needing any further persuasion, the three of us dived down into the awaiting darkness. Rocks whisked past us and the tunnel soon began to fill with thick, gritty dust. It stung my eyes and burnt my throat and lungs, but still I raced on. The shaft made a hideous cracking noise as if the very core of the Earth was being ripped open. The dust and falling rock had now become so dense that I had lost sight of Kayla and Isidor and I couldn't even call out for fear of sucking in a lungful of the burning dust that was now suffocating me.

So, with my arms held out before me, I lent further forward, mimicking the shape of an arrow and raced forward at a blistering speed. The wind rushed past me, my hair bellowed back from my brow, and my wings fluttered so furiously that I couldn't even see them. Peeking through my long eyelashes, I snatched a look at those little black claws that had repulsed me so much and could see that they were batting away rocks that were heading towards me. They moved with a nimbleness and speed that was mesmerizing to watch as they plucked rocks out of the air and tossed them out of harm's way. They were protecting me and I wondered if they were something that should be feared after all.

Closing my eyes against the grit and dark, I could feel the pressure of the falling debris behind me, and to my horror, I got the feeling that the shaft was actually becoming narrower. Why could nothing ever be easy for me? Just when I thought things couldn't ever get any worse, they usually did.

I feared that if I didn't reach the end of the shaft soon, the tunnel would collapse in all around me. Willing myself forward, I darted between lumps of rock, skirted past jagged outcrops that jutted from the shaft walls, and all the while the shaft became thinner.

As I panicked, I breathed deeper, and the deeper I breathed, the more of the burning dust I took in and I began to feel as if I were drowning - suffocating.

But I wouldn't be beaten - I couldn't be. So with the last of the breath I had within me, I tucked my arms tight against my body, lowered my head, arched my wings and just dropped like one of the rocks that soared past me. The fall was endless and just when I thought it was never going to stop, my heart suddenly leapt. There was a spot of orange light below me. I angled my body towards it. I don't know how long or how far I dropped, but I must have fallen hundreds of miles below the Earth's surface. As I fell, the orange light didn't seem to grow larger though, and at first I couldn't work out why. Surely, if I were heading towards it, the hole would start to become bigger. But this hole wasn't growing in size; in fact, it looked as if it were getting smaller! The hole – my escape from the shaft – was filling in with the rock and earth which had overtaken me.

Then in that little chink of light, I saw the silhouette of a figure and it appeared as if it were looking up and waving frantically at me.

Potter? I wondered as I felt myself begin to lose consciousness. *Potter, help me!* I wanted to call out, but I couldn't, I had no breath left in my lungs. I squinted through the falling dust and rock one last time at the orange light with the waving figure.

Then, all of a sudden, that figure was grabbing at me, pulling me out of the collapsing shaft and taking me into their arms.

"Potter?" I whispered.

"Shhh," the voice said, "It's me, Luke, I've got you. Welcome to The Hollows."

Chapter Nine

"General outer appearance of the deceased..." the voice said. It was female and seemed to echo off stone. The voice said something else but the darkness took me again and there was nothing.

"The deceased appears to be mildly decomposed..." the female voice said again. "It has obviously been left out in the open for approximately forty-eight hours. Maybe less, but no longer."

The voice was soft, but serious – professional. I swooned back from the darkness, my head feeling light although I could feel it resting against something hard and cold.

"Body is that of a female – approximate age early twenties..." the voice said and trailed off again as I slipped once more back into nothingness.

Surfacing again, I could feel fingers prodding me as if being examined by someone. The voice came again and I guessed that it was the owner of that soft, clinical voice who was performing some kind of inspection of me.

"The deceased has the first two index fingers intact on the left hand and the right has a thumb, forefinger and third index..." the female said.

"That's impossible!" said another voice – a male voice.

"Shhh!" the female said.

Ignoring her, the male continued: "When we pulled her off that mountainside, she didn't have any fingers! What you're trying to tell me is, they're growing back?"

"Photograph this," the female said to another who was in the room.

Above the darkness, a sudden burst of white light popped. It startled me. I wanted to flinch but I couldn't. I was paralysed. The female spoke again, and her voice came from above me, no longer sounding as if it were coming down a tunnel.

"The deceased is wearing black overalls, like combat clothing of some kind. On her feet she is wearing black boots.

Around her neck she is wearing a chain and silver crucifix..."

"Here, let me have those," the male voice said.

I felt my head being tugged at and my shoulders being lifted up off of whatever it was I was...

I'm lying down! I suddenly thought. They've laid me down! I tried to reach out and grab the hand that was removing the crucifix, but I couldn't. Although my brain commanded my arms to move, they refused.

Have they tied me down? I didn't think so, but my arms felt heavy and unmoveable.

The female spoke again. "The head is fully covered with flesh and it is bald except for a few partial hair fragments. There is no visible left eye socket – this is also covered with flesh. The right eye appears to be partially formed and has omitted what appears to be blood and a milky-type fluid. Please photograph this and take a few samples for DNA analysis."

The male cut in and his voice was riddled with confusion. "That can't be possible! She didn't have any eyes an hour or so ago!"

"You must be mistaken," the female said. "She couldn't be growing her eyes back. Could she?"

"You tell me! You're the pathologist!" The male said.

PATHOLOGIST! I screamed inside my head. That one word sent a stream of vivid images through my brain. My father had been a pathologist. I saw myself as if from above, looking down at the scene. Lying on a mortuary table...

That's why I'm lying down. The surface is hard and cold because it's made of metal...and the female is a pathologist, recording every detail of the body on the slab before she starts her...that's why she was prodding me...she's carrying out an external examination...that's why they're photographing me so she has pictures of my condition before she starts...the internal examination! "They think I'm dead! They're gonna open me up because they think I'm dead!" I screamed inside.

The pathologist continued her external examination, but her voice had changed. There was a tremor to it. All I could do was lay and listen.

"The deceased has no nasal cavity or nose. The cause of this is unknown at this time. The mouth is only partially formed..."

"She's growing a mouth now?" the male cut in.

"Shhh!" the female hissed. "If you can't keep quiet, I'll have to ask you to wait outside!"

"You can ask, lady, but I ain't going anywhere," the male spat. "I'm the lead police officer in this case and until I hear otherwise, I'm staying put. Look, I turned down a perfectly good steak 'n fri..."

"The deceased has no lips and the jaw line is swollen," the pathologist cut over him. "This is not the cause of death but may suggest that she was involved in some type of violent episode."

"So what is the cause of death?" I heard the police officer ask.

"Well, I think the fact that she's had her heart ripped out gives us a pretty good idea," the pathologist said dryly.

"So who is she?" the male voiced asked.

"I'm Kiera Hudson!" I wanted to scream at them.

Chapter Ten

"So you're Kiera Hudson? A voice asked.

I opened my eyes to see Coanda looking down at me. "Where am I?" I asked him, and I could still feel some of that rock dust in the back of my throat and between my teeth.

Handing me some water that came in a brown clay mug, Coanda said, "You're in The Hollows."

Sipping the water, which had a strange but sweet taste like candy floss, I looked about the small room that I now found myself in. It was lit by a series of small lamps that had been fastened to the walls. The room was in fact not a room at all, but more like a small cave that had been dug into the side of some giant red-coloured rock. There was a front door, and part of the room had been portioned off with a drab-looking curtain and from the bed that I was lying on, I couldn't see if anything was hidden behind it.

Across from me was a small wooden table which was covered with odd-looking maps and plans. Beside this table was a chair and Coanda lowered himself onto it. In the light of the lanterns, his face took on an almost florescent glow and his black, spiky hair appeared to shine like those models in the shampoo commercials. He was no longer stripped to the waist but wore a black combat-style jacket that was covered in a mass of pockets which bulged with whatever he had hidden inside them.

"Where are my friends?" I asked him. "Are they safe?"

"They're safe, for now" he said matter-of-factly.

"What's that supposed to mean?" I snapped, sitting up on the bed.

"Don't get yourself excited," Coanda said, waving at me to settle back down. They're quite safe. They are getting ready for the journey ahead."

"What journey?" I asked him. "How long have I been

unconscious?"

"Not long, just a couple of hours," Coanda informed me. "But long enough for me and my team to brief the others."

"Team? Journey? Briefings?" I groaned. "You're going to have to slow down."

With a smile that bordered on satisfaction spreading across his face, Coanda looked at me as if marveling some rare find and said, "Ravenwood told me you were feisty, strong-willed, a go-getter, if you like."

"What else did he tell you about me?" I asked, peering at him over the rim of the clay mug.

"That you were *the one*," he said, his eyes growing wide. "The one that would bring peace to The Hollows and stop the annihilation of the human race."

"As far as I can understand from the letter Ravenwood left me," I started, "One race, either the Humans or the Vampyrus, have to be annihilated, as you describe it."

"Ravenwood was right in what he told you," Coanda said, and he looked at me with his big, cold blue eyes. "One of the species has to cease to exist, but they can die without the suffering that war brings. As soon as you decide which race goes, they just fade away, like shadows. There will be no pain, no suffering for them."

Staring back at him, I said coolly, "I couldn't care what happens because I'm not making any choice. I refuse to be the one who wipes out an entire race of people."

Strumming his fingers against his thigh, Coanda looked at me thoughtfully and said, "I don't think you understand, Kiera..."

"No, it's you who doesn't understand," I said, placing the mug on the table with the maps. "I am not making any decision. I didn't ask for this."

"But Kiera, you have to," he said. "That's why you were chosen. A half-breed...half of each race...someone who can really see - feel - which species deserves to go on."

"I know of two other half-breeds you could have chosen," I snapped at him. "Why not let Kayla or Isidor make the decision?"

Looking at me as if I was failing to understand something, Coanda said, "Kiera, would you really want to pass such a burden to your young friends? Do you really think that either of them would want to...or be strong enough to make that choice?"

"What makes you think that I'm strong enough to choose?" I said, fighting the urge to scream at him.

"I don't think anything, Kiera," Coanda said calmly, "It's the elders who have chosen you."

"But why me?" I pushed.

Coanda shrugged at me and said, "You'll be able to ask them soon enough."

"How come?"

"That is the journey that we have to make," Coanda started to explain.

"Before I go anywhere with you," I said, swinging my legs over the edge of the bed and sitting up, "I want to know exactly who you are."

"Isn't Ravenwood's word enough?" Coanda asked, standing up.

"Let's just say I've got trust issues," I said with a wry smile. "Now tell me, why was there a locker back at that facility with your name on it?"

"Is it still there?" Coanda grinned as if remembering happier times. "I don't suppose you came across my flight goggles, did you?"

"Flight goggles?" I asked bemused and wondered if he wasn't just stalling me.

"Believe it or not, I used to be a Royal Air Force test pilot," he said, sitting again on the chair. "Not wishing to brag, but I was pretty awesome. Women love a test pilot you know," he said glancing up at me.

"Do they?" I said, cocking an eyebrow.

"Some do," he half-smiled. "I think it was the uniform and all the danger."

"Danger?" I asked him.

"Believe me, Kiera, I flew some of the most dangerous planes they secretly designed in that place," he began to explain. "See, that facility was once owned by the Military of Defense. It was a secret test site for experimental planes they were working on, it was my team's job to fly those machines that those crazy sons of bitches dreamt up. But being a secret Vampyrus, I had my own little secret, which gave me an advantage."

"Wings?" I cut in.

"You've got it," he smiled with a look of satisfaction. "I pushed those machines harder and faster than any other test pilot. I knew that if those planes broke up mid-flight, I could always just fly away." And he made a swooping motion in the air with his hands. "Humans have this fascination with wanting to be able to fly; I was interested to see if they could ever design anything that could fly as fast as I could. I got a reputation of being a bit of a madman, a risk taker, but they always let me be the first to test the machines that they dreamt up. But then everything changed. They got rid of the planes and started doing other sorts of tests there. Tests that I wanted no part of."

"What sort of tests?" I asked him.

"They were messing with DNA and trying to breed..."

"Half-breeds," I finished for him.

"You got it, Kiera," he said. "That's where I first met Doctor Hunt and Doctor Ravenwood. It didn't take them long to realise that the Vampyrus who had taken over the facility weren't interested in finding a cure for the half-breeds, but a way of enhancing their abilities to become some deadly race they could help to overrun the Earth with. As soon as we discovered what was being planned, both Ravenwood and Hunt left and I went back down into The Hollows."

"Didn't you try and stop them?" I asked him. "Destroy the work that they'd been doing?"

"Not at first," Coanda said, and he looked away as if ashamed. "But things started to change in The Hollows. There were rumours that Elias Munn was real, that he was behind the rise in crime in The Hollows, the murders, and steadily increasing lawlessness. Rumours started to spread that the humans were planning to come and ravish The Hollows, ruin it, and take whatever they could find; that our women and children would be taken back to the surface for their own perverted pleasures. But some of us knew this wasn't true. Those of us who had lived amongst the humans knew that they didn't even know of our existence. They were too busy killing each other to worry about a race of hairy winged freaks beneath them. But the lies were spread by Munn and his agents and those lies took root in the hearts of many Vampyrus. They started to hate the humans, even though most of them had never stepped foot above ground. But if you tell a lie often enough, it becomes the truth. So when Munn's agents started to spread the word that the Vampyrus should fight back, invade above ground before the humans got below ground, there was no shortage of volunteers to go to war. Most of the murders were blamed on the humans. The story spread that human spies were sneaking below ground and killing Vampyrus. But I knew that it wasn't true and there were plenty of others who felt the same way I did. The fear was and still is that if the Vampyrus attacked the humans, then they would counter attack and the wars that were fought thousands of years ago by our two races would come of age again."

"So what did you do?" I asked him, as I slowly learnt how Elias Munn had started his campaign against the humans.

"I went back above ground," he said as if the answer was an obvious one. "I went and sought out Ravenwood and Hunt."

"But why?"

"The last time I had seen them, they had been involved in trying to create a cure for the half-breeds that had been born out of the secret marriages between Vampyrus and their unsuspecting partners. I was hoping that their work had failed as I'd heard rumours that Munn and his agents wanted to use it to develop this super-breed as a weapon against the humans.

"I tracked them down to this vast manor house, where they had some sort of hospital wing hidden in the attic. There were children there - sick half-breed children. I begged them to stop what they were doing and it was then that Ravenwood and Hunt explained the true nature of their work."

"And what was that?" I asked him, my heart sinking as he

looked back at me.

"They were working on the cure just in case they ever needed to save you," he said. "When Hunt and Ravenwood had discovered what the Vampyrus were working on at the facility, they sought an audience with the Elders in the Dust Palace. And it was here that they learnt of how only one could undo the work that Elias Munn had set in place. They told Ravenwood and Hunt of how a half-breed would come who would bring peace to The Hollows. After explaining the burden that this half-breed would carry, the Elders ordered Ravenwood and Hunt from the Dust Palace, sealing the door to their kingdom, stating that it wouldn't be opened again until the half-breed came to them.

"Therefore, not knowing who this half-breed was or even if they had been born yet, every half-breed that was delivered sick, Hunt and Ravenwood tried to keep alive with the cure that they were so desperately working on. So while Hunt and Ravenwood played doctor and nurse in their makeshift hospital hidden in the attic, I returned to The Hollows and formed the resistance."

"The resistance?" I asked him.

"The Vampyrus who hadn't been deceived by Elias Munn's lies and believed that the Elders had let them down. I felt the same about them," Coanda said. "They sat back, entombed in their Dust Palace and let Elias Munn build an army. They stayed away and it was as if they had given up. But I couldn't do that. I couldn't just sit back and watch this Munn lead two worlds into war. So I gathered a small number of like-minded individuals. We were small in number at first. Then more men and women came, and we created small groups. We had spies that could provide us with first-hand intelligence; we built escape networks, like the one you crawled through to get here, Kiera. We dug holes and trenches that led us behind enemy lines so we could spy on what Munn was planning. More male and female Vampyrus came and we became known as the resistance. They came from all walks of life – there are teachers, artists, and I think there are even some priests who came to fight. We have Vampyrus above ground too – those who got themselves into positions of power to react when the attack above ground comes. We have a series of coordinated attacks planned to try and defeat Munn's armies. But you can change all that, Kiera – you can make a choice."

Looking across the small cave-like room, I said, "I can't make that choice, Coanda. I can't be responsible for wiping an entire race from the Earth and from history. I will not do it."

"Then war it is, Kiera Hudson," he said matter-of-factly.

"There has to be another way," I whispered.

Ignoring me, Coanda stood as if readying himself, and looking down at me he said, "We leave tonight for the Dust Palace, the Elders are expecting you. But first we have to go to the Light House."

"The Light House?" I asked him. "Why would you need a light house? We must be hundreds of miles below ground."

"Believe me, Kiera, below ground gets very dark," he smiled, his eyes shining bright. "The Light House is at the very core of The Hollows. We've received word from our spies in the Dolce region that Munn's agents have captured the Light House."

"What's so special about this light house?" I asked confused.

"It is like a beacon," Coanda explained. "It shines its light throughout The Hollows. It turns at the same speed as Earth and its light creates our nights and our days, just like the Earth spins around your Sun. As the Light House turns, the regions of The Hollows that are caught in its light celebrate day and those caught in its shadow celebrate the night."

"So why has Munn's armies taken it over?" I asked, somewhat in awe of what Coanda had just told me.

"They are going to use it to coordinate their attack above ground," Coanda said, with a grim look. "Through its waves of light, they are going to give the orders to attack. They will use echo waves…"

"Is that similar to echolocation?" I asked him, trying to get my head around what he was telling me.

"Similar," he said. "One of the greatest senses we Vampyrus have is that of hearing. It doesn't work like human hearing – we hear in vibrations and waves, like echoes. Munn is therefore going to send messages out in the pulses of light that come from the Light House. In that way, he can have complete control over his armies that are spread around the world, just waiting to attack. But there is one who has the heightened sense of hearing – hearing like no other Vampyrus."

Knowing immediately who he was talking about, I said, "Kayla?"

"That's right," Coanda said. "We want to take her to the Light House and listen to the waves that are being sent out. We can't get close enough ourselves as the very vibrations of our movements will be detected and the alarm will be raised that we are close. But with Kayla, we could be some miles away and we are hoping she will be able to listen into the messages, those instructions and orders that are being beamed out to Munn's armies."

"Will it be dangerous for her?" I asked him, hoping for a straight answer.

"We will be with her," Coanda assured me. "Once we know their final plans, we will make our way to the Dust Palace and if you still refuse to make your choice and we do end up at war, then at least we will know their plan of attack and have an early advantage against Munn."

"But I can't ask her to put herself in danger," I told him firmly. "Kayla has been through too much already."

"Then make your *choice*, Kiera Hudson," he snapped at me.

"And this can end – there will no more war!"

"And what if I chose the Vampyrus to die?" I barked back.

"That means you die!"

Shrugging his shoulders, he looked straight into my eyes and said, "Either way, I'm dead. You don't think this is a war we can win, do you?"

Looking away, I said, "There has to be another way."

Sighing, Coanda went to the wooden door which led from the cave, and looking back at me he said, "There are some fresh clothes for you behind that curtain. Get yourself changed; we're heading for the Light House.

Standing, I went over to the curtain, but before I'd had the chance to pull it back, Coanda said, "Kiera, keep the reason we are going there to yourself. Don't tell anyone."

"Not even Kayla?" I asked, looking back over my shoulder at him.

"Not even Kayla," he said sternly. "One of your friends is a spy and that's the truth whether you believe it or not."

"But you can't suspect Kayla," I gasped.

"No, I don't," Coanda said. "But if this spy finds out why we are going to the Light House, they might not want her to make it and you will undoubtedly be putting her life in great danger."

Then, before I could say anything back, he swung open the wooden door and was gone, closing it behind him.

Chapter Eleven

Behind the curtain, I found a large bowl of water, a rough-looking sponge and a neat pile of clothes that had been placed on a chair along with a towel.

Kicking off my boots and removing my clothes, I dipped the sponge into the water and washed the grime and dirt from me. The fall through the drop shaft had left me covered in black soot and dust. The water was lukewarm, but it was better than nothing. The sponge wasn't like a sponge at all really – not like the ones I had in my bathroom back home in Havensfield. This was harder, coarse, and was more like some kind of wild plant. It had a mint smell that was at least refreshing.

I toweled myself dry and put on the clothes that had been left for me. I looked down at myself in the black overalls, which looked like I was just about to take part in some kind of guerrilla warfare. In a way, I guess that was what I was about to do. There was a belt and I tied it around my waist. Rummaging through my old coat pockets, I found my iPod and Murphy's crucifix. I put the iPod into one of the many pockets that covered my combat-style overalls and hung the crucifix around my neck.

For luck! I thought to myself.

Stepping from the other side of the curtain and back into the small cave, my head rocked back as a bright light went off in my mind like a firecracker. In that brief explosion of light, I saw myself laid down somewhere, dressed exactly as I was now. But there was a voice and it was as if it was coming from way off.

"I will now carry out an examination of the teeth, starting with the upper left side," the voice said. *"Eight present. Seven present. Six missing. Five missing. Four present...Wait a minute! The deceased has fangs!"*

Then the voice was gone and so was the bright light. Leaning forward, I reached for the door to the cave to steady myself, as fragments of a dream scattered themselves across the front of my mind. But deep inside, a cold chill ran through me. In that dream, I knew that I was dead.

Shaking my head to clear those thoughts and fears, I pushed open the door and any thought of dying faded in an instance as I got my first proper look at The Hollows.

I don't even know how to start describing it. I sucked in a breath, dazzled by the sheer radiance of the world that the doorway from the cave had opened into. The ground was covered in a thick carpet of what I can only describe as a lime green moss. It was soft and spongy, like walking on a deep-pilled carpet. There were trees, thousands of them. They looked as if they had been planted in the ground upside down. Their trunks were the colour of burnt embers and they stretched upwards like frail arms. Vines hung from them, and were coloured red, yellow, orange, and so many more. It was like being in New England during the autumn, only the colours were way more intense, almost blinding. I looked up and there seemed to be no end. It was like staring up into the reaches of the highest cathedral. Giant granite rocks spiraled heavenward. They almost seemed to entwine with each other, forming pillars that supported the world I now found myself in. The sky, if that's what it was called, seemed to twinkle with life, with the brightest stars on the darkest of nights. I stared up at them and realised that they were not stars at all but the pointed tips of stalagmites that hung down from above. There were millions of them. My description is in adequate, but there are no words I know of which could describe the sheer wonder and beauty of The Hollows. But there was a feeling too; the whole place felt as if it was charged with electricity in some way. It tingled – it was alive – if that makes sense. I could remember Potter telling me as we had lain in each other's arms in the caves beneath the Fountain of Souls, how beautiful The Hollows were; but 'beautiful' seemed like such an insufficient word. I doubted there was a word that could describe The Hollows.

Why would anyone want to leave this place, I wondered. Why would the Vampyrus want to poke their head above ground for the briefest of seconds when they lived in such wonder? But more importantly, how could I ever make the decision to destroy it?

In the distance there was a large open area of that lime green moss and it was covered for as far as I could see with tall structures made of red rock. There were rows upon rows of them, and caves had been carved in each one. They were the strangest looking apartment blocks I had ever seen. Male and female Vampyrus soared between them, and they looked preoccupied and even sad as if they were all deeply troubled. How could such looks of sadness be possible? But as I watched them, I guessed that these were members of the resistance that Coanda had gathered and they were preparing to defend themselves against Munn. So, however beautiful their world was, a great shadow had been cast over it for them.

Some of them swooped up into the sky and spread their wings. They flew in formation as if practicing and practicing for the hour they would have to take to the skies and defend their lives, their homes, their Hollows. I watched breathless as they soared up amongst the stalagmites, then come sweeping down again. Their wings reflected the light from the stalagmites' tips and they shimmered. They looked like angels – no gods – and that's what they were. And in my heart, I suddenly realised Elias Munn's desire to be above ground. These creatures were too beautiful, glorious, and wonderful to be hidden.

But weren't humans just as beautiful in their own way? Weren't they angels too? Sure, they couldn't fly, but they were just as magical in their own right. Didn't humans have an overwhelming desire to strive onwards, to better themselves? Weren't they also capable of creating great works of beauty, art, music, writing, and so much more? Didn't humans have a wonderful capacity for kindness, to love and find great joy in the world around them? Couldn't the Earth look beautiful too? There was good and bad in every race, and with tears spilling onto my cheeks, I was dreading the hour when I was going to be asked to make a choice between the two of them.

Chapter Twelve

"Why are you crying?" someone asked, and I looked round to see Luke coming towards me. We were dressed identically, in black overalls and boots. His dark hair was swept back from his brow, and his green eyes shone as brightly as the moss beneath my feet. Thankfully, he had shaved his tatty beard off and he looked so much better.

Wiping the tears from my face with the backs of my hands, I said, "It's just that this place is so beautiful, why would anyone want to bring war here?"

"I guess not everyone sees it with your eyes, Kiera," he said, gently wrapping his arm about my shoulder and pulling me close.

"They see it differently then?" I asked him.

"They just don't see its beauty anymore," he said softly.

"That's so sad," I whispered.

"Do the humans still see their world as beautiful?" he asked me. "Do they not take their world for granted? Aren't they destroying it day by day, hour by hour? Maybe that is both the Vampyrus' and the humans' failure."

"What is?" I asked, looking at him.

"That both species are flawed," he said. "We both destroy ourselves."

"I can't accept that," I told him. "There is good in people – both human and Vampyrus."

"Is there any good in this Elias Munn?" he asked me. "Aren't we on the brink of war because of that man?"

"If there is good in him, I will *see* it," I said.

"And how will you *see* it?" Luke asked his eyes wide as if not quite believing what I was saying.

"Because he could've killed me already and he hasn't," I told him.

"So why hasn't he?"

"Because he's in love with me," I said thoughtfully.

"In love with you?" Luke asked, sounding shocked. "How can he be in love with you? He doesn't even know you."

"I think he does," I said, staring back at him.

"Who is he then?" Luke said, sounding almost angry. "Tell me who Elias Munn is and I'll rip his heart out right now!"

"You can't take his heart, Luke," I said.

"Why not?" and I could sense the frustration in his voice.

"Because if he does love me, then there is good in him," I said. "No one can truly love another if their heart is solely full of hate."

"Don't tell me you are seriously going to try and reason with this guy?" Luke snapped.

"What choice do I have?" I asked, looking into his eyes. "There is no way I will choose between the Vampyrus and the humans. If this Elias Munn has love in his heart, then he can be saved and there will be no need for war, no need for him to -"

"Kiera!" Luke barked. "You can't be serious? Firstly, you have to love this guy too, that's how love works – true love."

"And what's the second reason?" I pushed him.

Breaking my stare and looking away, Luke said softly, "The second reason is that I love you, Kiera."

"Please, Luke…" I started.

Then turning to look at me again, Luke said, "Why can't you say it, Kiera?"

"Say what?"

"That you love me," he replied, his eyes losing their glow.

I looked away.

"Is there someone else?" he pushed.

I couldn't answer him.

"My God, you're saving yourself for this Elias Munn, aren't you?" Luke gasped. "You think that you can stop all of this and lift the burden you carry by giving yourself to him. But you have to love him back, Kiera and if you do, you'll give him the power to make the decision for you!" Then taking my hand, he looked into my eyes and said, "Kiera, let's run from this place together. We'll hide, have a life together. Let them have their war – it doesn't have to affect us. We could be happy together. You might not love me right now, but I know you have feelings for me, I've felt them. How can you possibly know your true feelings? You've been through so much. But away from here,

65

from all of this, your feelings might become clearer. Please, Kiera, let's run away together and get as far from here as possible."

Slipping my hands from his, I looked into his sad eyes and said quietly, "Luke, I don't run away from anyone or anything, it's not my style."

Stepping away from me, Luke gave me a half smile, but I could see fear beneath it. "You've already fallen in love with Elias Munn, haven't you?"

"Don't be ridiculous," I sighed. "I don't even know him." Then turning away, I saw Potter leaning against one of those upturned trees and he was staring at me.

I went towards him, but on seeing me approach, he flicked the cigarette away that had been dangling between his fingers and walked away.

"Potter!" I called after him, but he didn't stop, he didn't even look back.

I turned back towards Luke, but he had gone too.

Chapter Thirteen

"Kiera!" someone shouted, and I looked over my shoulder to see Kayla running towards me. She was with Isidor and she had a look of wonder and excitement splashed across her pretty face.

"Isn't this place amazing?" she cried. "Have you ever seen anything like it?"

"No," I said shaking my head and smiling at her.

"Isidor has been telling me all about where he grew up," she almost seemed to squeal with pleasure. "You're going to take us there, aren't you Isidor?"

"Sure," he said, then he looked at me. I could see in his eyes that he didn't look as happy about being back in The Hollows as Kayla did at discovering them.

"What's wrong?" I asked him.

"Nothing," he replied with a shake of his head. "It's just weird being back, that's all."

"Aww, take no notice of him, Kiera," Kayla beamed. "he just doesn't want to share this amazing place with anyone."

"It's not that," Isidor told her.

"What is it then, grumpy?" Kayla teased.

Looking about him, Isidor said thoughtfully, "The place just feels different than how I remembered it. It feels tense, like there is something bad coming."

I didn't know if Isidor could sense something different as this was my first time in The Hollows, but I knew he was right about something bad coming. Before he'd had the chance to explain further, we were joined by Coanda.

"Ready?" he asked us, but was staring at me.

"Sure," I said.

"For what?" Kayla asked me.

Glancing at Coanda and remembering what he had told me, I said, "We are going to make our way to the Dust Palace. I'm going to meet with these Elders and see if we can't figure a way out of this mess."

"The Elders will never see you," Isidor warned. "The Dust

Place is sacred ground. No one is welcome there unless they are invited.

"She's been invited alright," Coanda said dryly. "I wouldn't be surprised if they didn't roll out the red carpet for her."

"What's so special about you?" Kayla asked me.

"I'll -" I started, but Coanda cut over me.

"Explain on the way," Coanda finished. "We don't have time to lose. My spies inform me that Elias Munn has already set off for the Dust Palace."

"He definitely won't be invited in," Isidor said.

"If he goes with an army, he won't need to be invited in," Coanda said, "He'll just break down the door. Now let's get moving."

We left the resistance camp behind and Coanda briefed them to wait for his signal. Heading out through the upturned trees, the soft, covered ground soon gave way to a harder, rocky road that spiraled away into the distance. The road cut across a vast and desolate-looking land. It was red and arid, totally unlike the camp we had left behind. It reminded me of pictures I had seen on the internet that had been beamed back to Earth by exploration vehicles sent to Mars.

It was just turning dusk, and I pictured the Light House turning away from us, but its light still burnt fiercely on the horizon ahead, spinning its golden rays between the tips of two ragged mountains.

"What are those mountains called?' Kayla asked Isidor as we walked together.

"They're called The Weeping Peaks," he said.

"The Weeping Peaks," Kayla mused. "They sound nice."

"Do they?" Isidor said, and I detected a note of dread in his voice. Then he sped up just slightly, just far enough not to have to engage in any further conversation with Kayla. Perhaps he wanted to be on his own.

The sight of the landscape was awe inspiring and even though I had seen and experienced so much over the last several months, the realisation that I was now racing across The Hollows filled my heart with inspiration. I tried to absorb every detail, every shard of light that glinted through those mountains and every rock that glowed like embers on the surface of this incredible world. I looked back at the way we had come, and in the distance I could see the tops of those upturned trees glistening. Some distance away, I could see Potter and Luke. I couldn't tell if they were talking, but they walked apart.

"The Hollows is beautiful, don't you think?" Kayla asked, her voice soft.

"Mmm?" I said thoughtfully as I stopped watching Luke and Potter and faced Kayla again.

"The Hollows are amazing, aren't they?" Kayla said again.

"Incredible," I replied, as I watched the jagged scenery slip into the shadows cast by the revolving Light House.

"So why are the Elders expecting you?"

Over the next couple of hours as we walked towards the Weeping Peaks, I told Kayla everything I had read in the letter Ravenwood had left for me. I explained to her all about the history of Elias Munn and how he despised the human race because he had been rejected by one of them. Kayla thought Munn's story was tragic and sad. I told her about the importance of the half-breeds and one in particular, me. As I explained to her the decision I had been born to make, and how whichever one I chose to survive, we would take on that species form permanently, Kayla took my hand and I saw tears spill from her eyes and slide silently down her face.

"Why are you crying?" I asked her gently.

"I don't want to change, Kiera," she said. "I want to stay as I am."

"But I didn't think you liked being a half-breed – you know, with how you used to be bullied and everything," I said.

"That was back then," she sniffed. "That seems like it happened to a different person. I've just gotten used to the idea of who I really am – I don't want to go through anymore changes."

"So if you had to choose," I asked her, "What would you do?"

Then slowing, she looked me straight in the eye and squeezed my hands with hers. "Kiera, I'd rather die than make that choice." She walked away, and I watched the dying light shine off her flaming hair.

No pressure then, I thought to myself and walked on, lost to my thoughts.

We walked until it grew dark, my head down. Then without even noticing at first, we had drawn close to the foot of the Weeping Peaks.

"Why have we stopped?" I asked Coanda.

"This is as far as we go by road," he said, as both Potter and Luke sauntered towards us. They reminded me of two naughty school boys who were sulking because they'd had their toys confiscated.

Coanda waited for them to catch up then said, "Let's get going. We have a mountain to climb!"

Potter glanced at me then up at the mountain. He then made his way towards it. I looked up at the first Weeping Peak which stretched so far into the sky, that more than half of it seemed lost to darkness.

"Welcome to the Weeping Peaks," Luke said, and brushed past me.

"We've really got to climb that?" Kayla asked breathlessly.

"Indeed we have, so the sooner we get going the better," Coanda grinned.

"Can't we just fly?" Kayla sighed.

"No. We can't risk being tracked by echolocation," he snapped, then started to climb.

Kayla and I went after him, followed by Isidor, who still seemed quiet. The gradient of the mountain wasn't steep like I had expected it to be, but was more like climbing a hill. Coanda stormed ahead.

As we climbed, the last of the light faded as night drew in all around us. With it came a chilly wind that whipped up a blanket of rusty-coloured dust. We climbed for what seemed like hours, and my stomach began to rumble with hunger. And it was then that I realized that since being in The Hollows, I hadn't craved human flesh. I wondered if that was the same for Kayla and Isidor.

After a few more hours of walking, Coanda stopped ahead

of us. He had come to rest on a jagged piece of rock that jutted out from the side of the mountain. Rubbing his huge hands together, he looked at us as we gathered around him and said, "We'll take some rest here for a few hours and start again at dawn."

I watched Potter and Luke walk away from each other like two fighters preparing to duel at first light. Both slumped against some nearby rocks. Luke lay on his side, and using his hands as makeshift pillows, he closed his eyes. Potter took a cigarette from his pocket, lit it, and then looked at me as he blew smoke up into the night. Isidor and Kayla lay on the ground nearby and snuggled close to one another next to a fire that Coanda had started. Wanting to be alone, I walked some distance away. I lowered myself onto the ledge of a nearby rock. Stretching out on the ground, I winced at the pain in my calf muscles. The walk had been a long one and my eyelids felt heavy with tiredness.

Taking my iPod from my pocket, I thumbed through the tracks. Putting in the earphones, I rolled onto my side and fell asleep listening to *Run* by Leona Lewis.

Chapter Fourteen

"I've had my heart ripped out!" I wanted to scream at her. But just like my arms had refused to move, so did my mouth. I could feel the words working their way up the back of my throat, but they had become entangled around my tonsils and just couldn't free themselves.

Then I felt a finger force its way into my mouth. It wiggled up and down then left and right. It prodded my tongue and it tasted of rubber.

"I can taste rubber!" I screamed inside. "Please don't cut me open! I can taste rubber! You can't open me up if I can taste rubber!"

The finger ran itself over my teeth and I realised it was covered with a surgical glove.

Of course she'd be wearing gloves! She's doing a medical examination. They can be messy especially when it comes to cutting...

The pathologist continued her examination of me and said, "Teeth present. I will start with the upper left side. Eight present. Seven present. Six missing. Five missing. Four present...wait a minute...!"

I didn't know if it was the sound of her soft voice counting backwards, but I could feel my head floating again, falling backwards...falling backwards into darkness. The nothingness took me again.

I woke. Not in the very sense of the word. I woke up inside. My mind was awake again, but I wasn't sure if my body had woken. But this time my awakening was different. Everything was red. The world was covered in a red film. There were shadows and these were red too. The shadows took on forms and shapes. They were people. One lent over me. She was female. Her hair was pulled back into a ponytail and her face looked flushed scarlet. Her hands were covered in rubber gloves and they looked pink. At first I thought they were covered in blood...

My blood?

Then, I realised it was just the red film of blood covering my eyeball that was making them that colour. I managed to swivel my eye in its socket and the red got darker almost black. Then three thoughts hit me at once.

I can move my eye! And the red is blood. I can move my eye and it's covered with blood! And it's cold...why is it so cold?

Swivelling my one good eye, I tried to look down the length of my body. I couldn't see my toes, but I could see my chest and that was enough.

I'm naked! They've removed my clothes! Why have they taken off my clothes?

The pathologist spoke again. "Moving down the body, all internal organs seem to be intact apart from the heart." She prodded my abdomen with her pink glove and continued. "There are no signs of bruising, puncture wounds, or lacerations, apart from those above her left breast."

Through the red haze, I watched her turn to another shape in the corner. "Can you take a sample for blood group analysis?" she asked the shape.

The shape moved towards me, needle in hand.

"Please no needles. I hate needles!" I shouted inside.

I looked at the shape that came towards me. I couldn't tell if I had been stuck with a needle, all I could feel was coldness. I looked at the male working on me and guessed he wasn't the owner of the voice I had heard earlier. Hadn't that voice said he was a police officer?

Police officers don't take blood samples. I knew that because I used to be one. My thoughts were broken by the sight of something bright and gleaming passing in front of my field of vision. It looked sharp – pointed.

What was that?

Then the pathologist said, "I'm now going to start the internal examination. Is everyone in the room happy?"

"HAPPY?" I screamed inside. "YEAH I'M OVER THE FREAKING MOON! YOU'RE ABOUT TO OPEN ME UP AND...

"Wait a minute!" The police officer said. "I think I saw her eye move!"

"Impossible!" The pathologist said. "I've checked for all vital signs of life and..."

"I think you'd better check again, sweetheart," the police officer's voice came again, this time from the right-hand side of me.

"Yeah that's right! LOOK! LOOK! My eye's moving!" I yelled inside and moved my eye frantically from side to side and as I did the enormous shape of the police officer appeared like a giant red shadow beside me.

"Oh Sweet Jeezus!" The police officer hollered. "She's alive I'm telling ya!"

"Yes! Yes!" I'm alive I wanted scream but...

Chapter Fifteen

...a hand fell over my mouth and I woke with a start. It was pitch-black and I was cold. With my heart thumping in my chest, I stared through the darkness and could see Potter leaning over me, his hand clasped over my mouth.

"Shhh!" he whispered in my ear. "I want to show you something."

Gently, he removed his hand from over my mouth.

"What in the hell..." I started.

Then placing his forefinger against his lips, he stared hard at me and said, "Shhh!"

Taking me by the hand, he pulled me to my feet. I placed my iPod into my pocket and went with him.

I followed him in silence until we were far enough away from the others to not be overheard. I then asked, "Where are you taking me?"

"I want to show you something," he whispered back at me.

"What?"

"You'll see when we get there," he said, leaping from the side of the mountain and dragging me with him. We plummeted into the night sky, opening our wings and soaring into the night.

"We shouldn't be flying," I said as I glided next to him. "Coanda said that the Vampyrus could pick us up using their echo -"

"The guy's a Muppet," Potter grinned back at me. "It's not far, and if we keep low we should be okay."

"But..."

Then Potter was banking away so I followed. We skimmed just inches over the red, hard-panned landscape. Dust blew up in our wake, and my hair tossed out behind me. In the distance I could see an orange glow, like a crack in the night. As we drew closer, the crack grew bigger and it no longer looked like a mere split but an opening in the centre of the Earth. We raced towards it and the air grew warmer.

Potter began to slow, and I spread my wings to keep

alongside him. Arching his wings back, Potter hovered in the air, then taking hold of my hand, we gently floated towards the ground.

Leading me over to the giant fracture in the rocky ground, I watched as bright orange lumps of what looked like molten lava shot up into the night like a series of fireworks. Taking me towards the very edge, the air blew hot and arid. Dust swirled around us and it was as if we had become separated from the rest of the world. I looked at him, and his rugged looks glowed red and orange from the light that seeped from the abyss beneath us.

"Where are we?" I breathed, feeling breathless at the sight before me.

"A promise is a promise," he smiled back at me, and I loved that smile. It wasn't his cocky smile, the one I'd so often wanted to wipe from his face, but it was the nice smile – the one that I had so often wanted to kiss, the one that made my heart race.

"What are you talking about?" I asked him.

"Remember in the caves beneath that fountain I told you about that canyon?" he asked me. "Talles Varineris. I made you a promise that one day I would take you to see it. Well, this is it."

I looked down into the abyss, and it was like staring down into an erupting volcano. Red, yellow, and orange lava bubbled, hissed, and spat way below me.

Taking a deep breath, Potter said, "The canyon runs for miles, it's a fracture that runs across the centre of the Earth. Like I told you before, some Vampyrus have undertaken expeditions to try and find its start and its end, but none ever returned. Some say that they fell in or went mad and got lost in the millions of gorges and tunnels that twist and turn through the Talles Varineris."

Unable to take my eyes off the sight before me, I said, "I remember you telling me that if you stand right out on the very edge and stare down into the canyon, it's like looking into the Earth's soul. I didn't know what you meant back then, but I do now." I continued to watch the lava shift and move below as it took on the most incredible shapes of beauty. It was like my mind was playing tricks on me. The flames looked like horses galloping through hot orange waves, dolphins diving up into the air then melting into a spray of boiling lava. It shifted and rolled, and it was as if I could see all of Earth's creations bathing in the great, writhing sea of lava below. It was like the whole of creation had started down there in its depths and with each plume of lava that shot up into the air, it carried the spirit of that creature up into The Hollows, soaring higher through the layers of the earth and above ground.

"Enough already," Potter suddenly said, taking my arm and pulling me back from the edge of the canyon. "I told you that many have gone mad, mesmerized by what they see down there."

"But..." I started looking back over my shoulder at it, just wanting one last glimpse of its beauty.

"That's a sacred place down there," Potter said, turning my face in his strong hands. "It's to be respected, not understood."

Looking at him, I said, "You told me you came here with your mother and father."

"Yes," he said, looking away. "I don't have many good memories of them, especially not my father. But this place seemed to ease his temper somehow."

"You have a temper, Potter," I said, now turning his face back to look at mine.

"What's got into you?" he suddenly asked. "You've barely said two words to me since I came back from rescuing Luke."

"Im scared of you," I told him, as the sky lit up with jets of molten lava.

"Scared of me?" he scoffed. "Why would you be scared of me?"

"Why did you kill Eloisa?" I asked him straight out. The time for misunderstandings and untruths had passed. I wanted him to be honest with me.

"To get back at Jack Seth for playing his part in the death of Murphy," he growled at me.

"I don't believe you!" I yelled. "Stop lying to me!"

"She was a child killer, Kiera!" he shouted back. "Isn't that enough of a reason?"

"It isn't the reason why you killed her and I know it!" I raged at him, clenching my fists by my sides.

"What part of being a child killer do you not understand!" he roared, and the veins on his neck stood out like wires running beneath a carpet. "For hundreds of years, Eloisa and her kind have snatched children from their beds, strangled them, disemboweled them, fed on them, then discarded them like pieces of litter. For fuck's sake, Kiera, stop being so naïve. She was nothing but child-murdering scum and she deserved to die."

"Not like that," I said, staring at him. "Not to have her heart ripped out and chucked on the floor at the feet of Seth. No one deserves to die like that."

"That's how Murphy died!" Potter almost seemed to scream at me. "Jesus, Kiera, you just don't get it, do you!"

"Get what?" I hollered at him.

"You've never known what it's like to have your father punch you in the side of the head and tell you that you're a worthless piece of shit and that you would never amount to anything. You've never known what it's like to see your father come home and beat up on your mum, to have to listen to her screams coming from the bedroom while you lay in bed feeling helpless. Murphy was more like a father to me than my own ever was."

I watched Potter throw his hands over his ears, as if he could still hear his mother's screams. In the glow of the light from the canyon, I saw tears glistening on his cheeks. Then, staring at me, he said, "That's why I killed her, because she murdered children, she took their innocence – she took their lives! And however much she claimed to have made amends for her past, you can never redeem yourself for doing something like that. So, I'm sorry if I scared you, Kiera, but however scared you felt seeing that, it couldn't come close to the fear she put into the hearts of the children she murdered."

I looked at him as he took his hands away from over his ears, his mother's screams now fading away. "I'm sorry," I said, going towards him.

Holding out his hand as if to stop me from coming closer,

Potter said, "Please, Kiera, just leave me alone."

Ignoring him, I took his hand in mine and lowered it. "I'm sorry," I whispered again.

"What do you care anyhow?" he asked, unable to look at me. "I'm just Potter, the hired muscle, the gopher, the joker in the pack."

"What's that supposed to mean?" I asked.

"I've seen you and Luke having your private little chats since he came back," he said. "I saw you walking hand in hand up that mountain."

"We weren't holding hands," I said.

"Whatever," he huffed, pulling away from me. "I won't stand in your way now that Luke's back. I know you're in love with him and who could blame you? I mean that guy is the only one I know who can get the shit kicked out of him and still look good enough to appear in an Armani commercial! And then there's me with the crooked nose from too many fights…"

"Will you just shut up before *I* break your freaking nose?" I hollered at him. "I don't love Luke. It's you I'm in love with, Potter!"

"Look, sweet cheeks, you don't have to let me down lightly, I can take it," he continued as if he hadn't heard what I just said.

"Potter, will you shut that mouth of yours for once and listen?" I screamed at him. "I love you!"

Then looking at me as if I had just punched him straight in his jaw, he said, "What did you just say?"

"I said, I love you. Even though you can be the most infuriating arsehole I've ever met, you smoke like a goddamn chimney, you're arrogant, foul-mouthed, and -"

"Okay, so they are all my good points," he cut in, "What don't you like about me?"

"You scare me," I whispered as he came close.

"I thought I explained that," he said.

"No, it's more than that," I said, looking into his eyes. "There's a darkness about you, but I'm drawn to it, even though I get the feeling that I'm going to get hurt. I can't help myself."

Then, pulling me against him, he said, "I won't ever hurt

you, tiger."

Before I had a chance to say anything else, he had covered my lips with his and we were sinking onto the ground as the night sky shone orange and red from the lava that created its beautiful shapes below.

Chapter Sixteen

The warm air rising from the canyon kept our naked bodies warm. I fumbled for my iPod in the pocket of my overalls which lay strewn across the ground where Potter had thrown them.

Handing it to him, I said, "Find us a song."

He took it from me and without saying anything, he scrolled down the list of songs. Then, placing it on the ground next to us, *Wonderwall* by Oasis started to play.

I lay on my back and looked up into the night sky. Plumes of lava sprayed up into the night like a fireworks display. Watching them create their magical shapes, I noticed what appeared to be two irregular-shaped moons shining brightly back at me.

Potter caught me staring at them and said, "They're pretty cool, aren't they?"

"Are they moons?" I asked him.

With his head tilted back, he spoke quietly as if he were in the presence of some great power. "We call them our moons, but in fact, they are two captured asteroids."

"Asteroids?" I asked confused. "Don't they belong in space?"

"It's what we call them. I guess they are just two old rocks that float around up there and no one really knows why. Asteroids sound better than just boring old rocks!" Then pointing up into the sky with one long finger, he added, "We call that one Phobos and the other Deimos."

"They're incredible," I agreed. "They are just as beautiful as the moon."

Potter remained silent as he continued to stare up at the two bright asteroids, or rocks, that bathed us in their milky light.

I thought about above ground and realised I had never looked at it in the same way I looked at The Hollows with its two moons. Perhaps I had taken my own home for granted. Perhaps it was as beautiful as The Hollows, but I had just never truly appreciated it.

"Above ground is beautiful too," I sighed thoughtfully, as the music continued to play.

Potter rolled onto his side, and brushing my hair from my face, he traced his fingers down the length of my neck, over my breasts, and laid his hand gently across the flat of my stomach. I looked at him and smiled, then stared again up at Phobos and Deimos again.

"Where do we go from here?" I whispered.

"Ask Coanda, he's the man with the plan," Potter said.

"I didn't mean that," I smiled back at him.

"What did you mean, sweet cheeks?" he muttered as he lightly kissed my neck, making my skin tingle.

Taking his hand from my stomach, my heart beginning to race, I asked, "Are you Elias Munn?"

"What?" Potter stammered, his eyes widening. "This is some kind of joke, right?"

"No joke," I said, staring back at him.

"Why would you even think that?" he asked, sounding more confused than angry.

"Elias Munn killed his lover by ripping her heart out," I told him.

"So?" Potter said, staring back at me, his eyes so black I could see the lava that was shooting up into the sky reflecting back in them.

"That's how you killed Eloisa," I whispered, breaking his stare.

"And that's how Phillips killed Murphy," Potter reminded me. "Perhaps he's this Elias Munn. Ever thought about that?"

"No," I whispered.

Pulling me close to him, he held me in his arms and said, "Kiera, I don't know where or how you got this crazy idea into your head, but I'm not *him*. I promise."

Then, looking up into his face, I whispered, "I'm scared, Potter."

"Why? I'll keep you safe," he tried to assure me.

"I don't need looking after," I told him softly. "I'm scared of this decision I've got to make. If I choose the Vampyrus to live, then the humans die and I can't do that. But if I choose them over the Vampyrus, then you die."

"Listen to me, Kiera, Ravenwood was just a crazy old man," he said. "Wait until we get to the Elders, they will tell you what the truth is."

"But it's not just Ravenwood's letter that spoke of this choice I have to make," I said. "There was someone else too."

"Who?"

"Coanda," I told him.

"Coanda is full of shit!" Potter groaned. "The guy thinks he's a freaking legend. Yesterday was the first time I met the guy, but I've heard the stories about him. He thinks he's the Evel Knievel of the skies!"

"But he's built this resistance..." I started.

"Resistance my arse!" Potter spat. "That's not a resistance - that's a bunch of fucking groupies! He's probably screwed half of them! The guy is an arrogant, womanizing, Biggles-wannabe. Don't listen to him."

"But..." I started, then stopped.

"But what?" Potter pushed.

"It's nothing," I said, looking away.

"Tell me, Kiera," Potter insisted. "What has he said? Or more importantly, what has he got planned?"

"He told me not to tell anyone," I told him.

"Where is he leading us?" Potter asked, his voice full of concern. "Kiera, listen to me, that guy has pulled so many crazy stunts in his time, he could have his own series of 'Jackass'. He could be leading us into a whole heap of shit!"

Turning to look at him, I said, "I promised him I wouldn't say anything, for Kayla's sake."

"Kayla!" Potter barked. "What has she got to do with this?"

"I can't...he told me not to trust anyone," I whispered.

"But it's okay to trust him?" Potter hissed. "That's rich coming from the guy who is so far up his own fucking arse he thinks he's one of the Wright Brothers! He's more like one of the Marx Brothers! The guy's a clown!"

I looked at Potter and he stared back.

"If you love me, Kiera, you will trust me," he pushed.

"He's taking us to the Light House," I whispered, fearing

that someone other than us might hear.

"The *Light House!*" Potter almost choked.

"Shhh!" I hissed, and glanced back over my shoulder.

"Are you taking the piss?" he asked in disbelief.

"No, that's where Coanda is leading us," I said.

"Kiera, this isn't like any ordinary lighthouse," he cried. "It's not tall and white, with a pretty-looking light on top and it isn't set on the shores of some beautiful coastline."

"What is this Light House like, then?" I snapped back.

"Your worst fucking nightmare, that's what it's like!" he hissed.

"I don't know so much, I've had some pretty intense nightmares lately," I told him.

"The *Light House* is a needle of rock that towers out of the ground."

"That doesn't sound so bad," I told him.

"When I say that it towers out of the ground," Potter said, "It juts out of the Earth's core! Coanda must be smoking crack if he thinks we can go to the Light House."

"Why?"

"We call that splinter of rock the Light House, because it reflects the light from the centre of the Earth, which, if you didn't know already, is a hideous, raging, inferno. The tower is unstable and floats on a whirlpool of burning, molten lava, and as it turns, it showers its light across The Hollows, creating day and night."

"Coanda explained that part to me," I told him.

"That was big of him," Potter scowled. "So, where does Kayla fit into all of this?"

"Coanda knows that she has heightened hearing," I explained, "So he wants to get as close enough to the Light House as possible."

"Why? What the fuck is he hoping to hear?"

"That's where Elias Munn is going to coordinate his above ground attack from," I told him. "He's going to send his orders by echo-waves via the light radiated from the Light House."

"So what's he planning to do, even if Kayla does hear some gem of intelligence?" Potter asked, sounding unconvinced.

"It will give him and the resistance a chance to outwit Elias Munn," I said.

"That is the craziest idea I've heard," Potter groaned. "It's not even an idea, its suicide and I'm not going to be a part of it and neither are you."

"Please," I said, "We've got to go along with it. Otherwise, Coanda will know that I've told you."

"But it could be a trap," Potter warned me. "Where did he get this information from?"

"One of the resistance who was spying on the Vampyrus," I tried to assure him.

"What about Kayla? We could be putting her in danger," he said, staring at me with his dead, black eyes.

"That's why we mustn't tell anyone what Coanda has planned," I warned him. "Please don't say anything."

Potter looked at the jets of lava that continued to shoot up into the night sky. Then, turning slowly to look at me he said, "Okay, I'll go along with it for now, but I'm warning you, Kiera, the first sign that we are heading into a trap and I'm walking - with or without you - and I'll be taking Kayla with me."

Chapter Seventeen

We arrived back at the camp just before the dawn – or before the Light House completed its cycle and started to spread its light over the Weeping Peaks.

Landing on the side of the mountain, Potter kissed me gently on the mouth, then we split, so if any of the others were awake, they wouldn't know we had left the camp together. I went back to my spot on the ledge that jutted from the side of the mountain, and closing my eyes, I drifted into a dreamless sleep.

Just before dawn, I was gently shaken awake. Opening my eyes, I could see it was Luke who had woken me.

"It's time we made a move, sleepyhead," he smiled down at me and I knew that he had chilled a little from the crossed words we had shared back at the resistance camp.

Looking up into his face, I knew that I couldn't put it off for much longer; I had to tell him about Potter and me. But how was I going to tell him that I had fallen in love with his best friend? I knew that it would hurt him. After all, he had saved my life on so many occasions, dived into a burning church, taken a beating in the caves below the mountain for me, and while he'd been imprisoned, I'd fallen in love with his best friend. However I told him, it was going to hurt.

Handing me another of those clay-type mugs, he asked, "Are you okay, Kiera?"

"I'm fine," I lied, taking a sip from the mug. The contents were warm and bitter, and I screwed up my face.

Laughing, Luke said, "You'll get used to the taste in time."

"What is it?" I asked, staring down into the yellow liquid that sloshed around the inside of the mug.

"Sloff," he said, as if that should mean something to me. Then, seeing the look of confusion on my face, Luke added, "It's like tea or coffee, I guess. Anyway, drink up. Coanda is keen to get moving."

Luke went to walk away, but before he'd gone too far, I called out to him. "Luke!"

Turning, he looked at me and said, "What's up?"

Making sure that I couldn't be overheard, I asked, "What do you make of Coanda?"

"A bit of a flyboy, but he's okay, I guess." Then he said, "Why do you ask?"

"No reason," I smiled back at him. "Give me five and I'll catch up."

Holding me in his gaze for just a moment longer, he finally turned and sauntered away. I took another sip of the Sloff, and turning up my nose, I ditched the rest of it over the side of the mountain.

I joined the others as Isidor was kicking ash over what was left of the burning embers. Potter stood on the other side of the camp and seemed protectively close to Kayla. He looked at me, but his face looked emotionless. He held my gaze as he stuck a cigarette in the corner of his mouth and lit it. I half-smiled back at him, then looked away.

Once Isidor had kicked out the fire, Coanda clapped his giant hands together and said, "Okay, let's get moving." He then turned and started back up the mountain.

"I don't want to be a pain in the arse, but where are we actually heading?" Potter called out after him.

I shot Potter a look, but he was staring at Coanda.

"We're heading for the Dust Palace," Coanda smiled back at him. "I thought I'd explained that, Potter."

"I might be wrong, as I've always been pretty shit at geography, but I thought the Dust Palace was more to the East. We seem to be heading more inland," Potter said.

"I know a different route," Coanda smiled again. "A safer route."

"Safer?" Potter mused as he chewed the end of his cigarette. "Are you expecting trouble then?"

"No trouble," Coanda said, and although he smiled, I could tell it was forced. Potter had rattled him, but then again didn't Potter rattle everyone?

"Just checking," Potter smiled back at Coanda. "Lead on."

Turning his back on us, Coanda marched off up the mountain.

I looked at Potter again and he winked at me, then headed off after Coanda, Kayla by his side. Isidor slung his crossbow over his back and set off too. He looked sullen as if he had the weight of the world on his shoulders. His head was hung low and he looked tired as if he hadn't slept too well. I didn't want to walk with Luke, not just yet, not until I knew how I was going to tell him about Potter and me, so I caught up with Isidor.

"How are you doing?" I asked him as we made our way up a path that spiraled around the outside of the Weeping Peaks.

"Fine," he said.

"Are you sure?" I pushed gently.

"Sure," he said back without looking at me.

"How are your cravings?" I asked.

"For human flesh, you mean?"

"Yes."

"Gone, but then again I always knew they would be once I came back home," he said.

"Are you glad to be home?" I asked him.

"I guess."

"So what's wrong?"

Turning on me, his little chin beard bristling in the breeze, he said, "How many ways have I got to tell ya, Kiera, there's nothing wrong." Then he was gone, striding ahead on his own.

"I'm sorry, Isidor," I called out after him, but he was gone, lost to his own personal thoughts, and I couldn't help but feel anxious about what was worrying him.

"Leave the boy be," someone said, and I looked back to see that Luke had caught up with me.

"I guess," I said, looking at Isidor, desperately not wanting to make eye contact with Luke.

"He's obviously got something on his mind," Luke said.

"You've noticed it too?"

"Whatever it is, he'll tell you when he's ready."

"I'm sure you're right," I sighed, stealing a quick glance at him.

Luke was looking at me and said, "Fancy walking together?

"Sure," I smiled at him. I didn't feel I could say no, even

though I wanted to.

"I'm sorry about yesterday," he said.

"Sorry for what?" I asked, although I knew exactly what he meant.

"Coming on heavy like that," he said. "It's just I can't help my feelings for you, Kiera."

Glancing sideways at him, I said, "You've got nothing to be sorry for, Luke."

"Have you thought any more about what I said?" he asked.

"Can't we talk about this another time?" I asked, desperate to avoid the issue.

"Sure," he said, looking a little embarrassed. "What do you want to talk about?"

"How did you get out of the zoo?" I asked him.

He paused for a moment as if a little surprised by my question. "I escaped."

"Yeah, I figured that out for myself, but how?" I pushed, interested to hear all about it.

"They had me held for months in this little cell beneath the zoo," he started. "At first I didn't even know that it was a zoo, not until I came above ground. They fed me the red stuff and I'm ashamed that I ate it – but I knew that if I were to ever rescue you and the others, I needed to be strong."

"I thought they had killed you," I told him. "After the beating you took in the caves, I feared that perhaps you were dead."

"I was already in pretty bad shape when those vampires dragged me from that lake," he said. "They were going to kill me, but Phillips said he wanted me alive to be used as a bargaining tool in case you refused to eat the red stuff. I guess that's why they never killed me in the zoo. Phillips and Sparky had figured out that we meant something to each other, that we were friends, and they knew they could use me."

"So how did you get out?" I asked him again, keen to see if his escape had been as grueling as mine.

"In the end it was easier than I thought it would be," he said. "They just opened up the doors."

"How come?" I was surprised to hear this.

"They just suddenly deserted the zoo and left," Luke told me. "But I knew why they had fled that zoo, something had scared them. I'd overheard two of the Lycanthrope talking about how some virus was loose in the zoo and some of the half-breeds had died. At first I panicked as I thought they were talking about you, Kayla, and Isidor. But within a matter of days, they had all left. I stayed in my cell for a few days more, and when on the fourth day those werewolves hadn't brought anymore of that meat to me, I realised I hadn't heard a sound from anyone in days. I knew that they had vacated the zoo. So, suspecting that no one was going to stop me or raise the alarm should they hear me, I tore down the cell door. It was only when I made it from the basement that I realised where I had been kept.

"My suspicions had been right, the zoo had been deserted. I searched every empty cage and cell for you and the others, but couldn't find you anywhere. Not knowing if Phillips and the others would return at any moment, I fled the zoo. But within moments of me escaping, a storm had started. Not too sure exactly where I was or what direction I should head in, and not wanting to fly for fear of being recaptured, I walked half-naked in the freezing snow. For hours I staggered blind through the blizzard until I became totally disorientated. When I thought I couldn't go on any further, I saw a shape in the distance coming towards me. Not knowing if I should draw attention to myself in the hope that I might be rescued, I hid behind an outcrop of nearby rocks. And like an apparition appearing out of the snow, I saw that it was Potter. Barely able to stand, I stumbled out from my hiding place and into his path.

"Potter took off his coat, and wrapping it about my shoulders, he led me to a nearby overhang set into the side of a hill. He lit a fire, skinned some rabbit, and we waited for the storm to ease. He said at first he hadn't recognised me through my long beard and hair. I owe him my life."

"Why do you think they abandoned you in the zoo like that?" I asked him. "Why not kill you before they fled, or take you with them for future bargaining opportunities?"

"At first I wondered if, in their haste to leave, they just

forgot about me sitting down there in the basement," Luke said. "Then I feared that perhaps you were dead, and that I no longer served any further purpose, so Phillips was happy to just leave me to starve to death. After all, who was going to rescue me?"

"Potter," I said.

"Exactly," Luke said, "And that was Phillips' mistake – he underestimated the power of true friendship. Potter and I are like brothers and I know he would never do anything to hurt me."

To hear Luke boast of his friendship with Potter made my heart ache. How was I ever going to tell him that his best friend had fallen in love with me and I had fallen in love with him?

Chapter Eighteen

We walked in silence. Not because Luke wanted to, but because I had nothing to say. I guess that's not exactly true; I had lots to say – stuff that I needed to tell Luke, but I just didn't know how. I didn't even know where to start. As we walked onwards up the mountain, in my mind I played out the hundreds of ways I could tell him how I felt about Potter and how he felt about me. But the only way was truthfully – Luke deserved that at least. When did I tell him, though? Because once something like that was out, there was no way of taking it back. How much longer did I put it off? I knew in my heart that time was running out.

Throwing Luke a sideways glance, I watched him as he walked silently beside me. His head was down, and he looked deep in thought. He knew that things weren't quite right between us – they weren't like they had been before. Would he ever be able to forgive me? But did that matter? What mattered more was if he would be able to forgive his best friend, Potter. He had already lost Murphy, and although he hadn't spoken about that, I guessed he couldn't face it. So much had happened while Luke had been locked away in the zoo. I could see the hurt in his eyes every time I looked at him, and I was just going to add to that hurt and deep down, I wondered if I could do it to him.

But to not tell him about Potter and me, however painful it might be, was unfair on him, so forming the words in my head, I gently touched him on the arm and said, "Luke, there is something I need to tell you."

Raising his head, he looked sideways at me and said, "Oh, okay. What is it?"

Before the words I had planned had reached my lips, Kayla came running up to us and said, "We're being followed!"

Staring at her, I asked, "Who's following us?"

"Dunno," she said, her eyes wide, almost scared looking.

"How can you be so sure?" Luke asked her.

"I can hear them," she said, tapping her right earlobe with the tip of her finger.

"What's going on?" Potter asked, coming back to join us.

"Kayla says we're being followed," I told him.

Looking at Kayla, then at Luke, Potter said, "C'mon, Luke let's go back and see if we can't find them."

"No!" someone said, and we all turned to see Coanda looking at us.

"I don't take orders from you," Potter snapped back at him.

"Listen to me," Coanda said, coming forward, Isidor just behind him, crossbow raised. "We keep moving forward and we don't split up. We will be safer together."

"But if we're being tracked..." Luke started.

"Then we lose them," Coanda said firmly.

"How?" Kayla asked.

"We go into the willows," Coanda said.

"Bad idea," Isidor said, and Coanda glanced back at him as if unaware that he was there.

"Why?" I asked, reading the concern, no, fear in Isidor's dark eyes. "What are the willows?"

"Haven't you asked yourself why these mountains are called the Weeping Peaks?" Isidor replied, his voice now no louder than a whisper.

"For crying out loud -" Potter started.

But this time, Isidor cut over him. "I couldn't have said it better myself, Potter. If we go amongst the willow trees, you will be crying out loud."

"Just a load of old hocus-pocus nonsense," Potter sneered. "You've listened to too many bedtime stories, kid."

Stepping towards Isidor, I said, "Take no notice of him. Tell me what happens amongst the willow trees."

"Some say they are haunted," Isidor started. "But not by ghosts."

"Then by what?" I pushed.

"All that has ever made you sad," Isidor said, staring into my eyes. "The willows are meant to evoke all those feelings of unhappiness you have ever felt."

Then coming forward to stand at my elbow, Potter lit a cigarette and said, "See, what did I tell you? Just a bunch of old crap!"

"We should go!" Kayla said, tugging at my sleeve. "Whoever is following us is close."

Turning and leaving the path, Coanda said over his shoulder, "If it's just a bunch of hocus-pocus, Potter, then you won't mind following us into the willows." Then he was gone, striding forward towards a dark shadow of trees that loomed in the distance.

Pitching out his cigarette, Potter looked at me and said, "Watch your back." And just like Coanda, he headed for the willows.

Looking back over her shoulder, Kayla said, "Whoever it is, their heartbeat has quickened. They're running!"

"In which direction?" Luke asked her.

"Ours!" Kayla breathed, setting off towards the trees.

With crossbow still raised, Isidor sniffed the air and said as if to himself, "I can smell them." Then, he was walking away after his sister, and Luke and I followed.

The trees leaned from the side of the mountain, forming a thick, wooded area that, from a distance, looked like a giant beast with many writhing tentacles. The drooping branches of the thousands of willow trees swung to and fro like leafy curtains. As we approached them, I couldn't help but be reminded of the crop of weeping willows that surrounded the children's graveyard on the grounds of Hallowed Manor, and to think of it made my flesh shiver with goose bumps.

Reaching the edge of the woods, I heard something, almost like a whisper on the breeze. At first I thought it was just the wind playing tricks with my hearing, but as I followed the others amongst the willows, I was sure I could hear the sound of weeping. The woods were dark, and very little light from the Light House penetrated through the overhanging branches of the trees. We walked in silence, Coanda always ahead of us, peeling back the branches with his muscular arms. The sound of weeping continued, and as we moved further amongst the willows, the sound of crying grew louder. It sounded like a nation of people crying out as if all were suffering the most terrible nightmare. The weeping was filled with sorrow and anguish; I just wanted to cover my ears with my hands to block it out.

I looked to my left and then quickly to my right only to find that I was on my own.

Where are the others? I wondered. *How had I been separated from them?*

"Potter?" I called out, but it was as if my voice had been drowned out – smothered – by the continual sound of crying.

Then, just ahead amongst the trees, I saw someone. "Hey!" I called after them. "Luke, is that you?"

The figure disappeared amongst the willows and I lost sight of it. Speeding up, I ran amongst the trees in search of the figure. With my heart pounding and the sound of sobbing all around me, I pushed the swinging branches aside like rows and rows of curtains. Then, just ahead of me, I saw the figure again. But this time, it stood motionless with its back to me.

"Hey you!" I yelled, desperate not to be alone in this place.

Hearing me call out, the figure turned and looked straight at me. With my legs almost buckling beneath me, I threw my hands to my face and drew a shallow breath.

Hooking his finger into the shape of a question mark, he beckoned me forward, then turning, he disappeared amongst the willows again.

"Dad!" I called out. "Dad wait for me!"

Chapter Nineteen

My first thought should have been, *"What is my dad doing here? He's dead, isn't he?"* but to see him again filled my heart with joy, so much so that I thought it was going to explode.

I raced between the trees to where he had been standing. "Dad!" I called after him. "Don't go, wait for me!" Reaching the spot where I had last seen him, I clawed back the branches of the tree to find him sitting against the trunk reading a book. Hearing the rustle of the branches, he looked up at me and smiled.

"Dad?" I breathed.

"Hey, Kiera," he said softly, placing the book open on the grass beside him. I looked down at the cover and could see that he had been reading his favorite book, *Hamlet* by William Shakespeare.

Going to him, I dropped to my knees and threw my arms around his neck. And all at once, the smell of him and the feel of his touch filled me with sadness and longing. All those feelings of loss I had felt since his death washed over me like a tidal wave. The times I had needed him, missed him, wished that he had been there for me, took hold of my heart and it felt like agony.

"Dad," I began to sob, and my own weeping joined the chorus of unhappiness that haunted this place. The joy I'd felt at seeing him had now vanished. "Dad, I miss you so much," I told him. Then he was gone, like vapor slipping from between my arms.

"Don't leave me again!" I cried. "I need you!"

Standing, I spun around on the spot, desperate to find him again. And there he was, sitting against the tree, his favorite book in his hand. Seeing me, he placed the book open on the grass just like he had done before. Again, my heart leaped with joy.

"Dad?" I whispered.

"Hey, Kiera," he smiled up at me.

Falling to my knees again, I hugged him tight. The smell of

Old Spice wafted beneath my nose, and my head swam with images of me on his lap as a child. Those feelings of being safe, secure, and loved came flooding back. I tried to hold onto them as tightly as I held him in my arms.

"Dad," I whispered against his cheek and it felt soft, freshly shaved. "I need your help. I have to make a decision – a choice – and I can't do it. I don't want to do it, Dad."

He remained silent in my arms, but I didn't want to let go just in case he disappeared again. With my tears dampening his cheek, I said, "Please tell me what to do."

Silence.

"Tell me how I should choose," I begged him.

Silence.

"Please tell me I don't have to make the choice," I sobbed. "If there is a way, let this decision I have to make pass me by. Take it from me."

Silence.

"Tell me who this Elias Munn is," I whispered through my tears. "At least tell me that."

Then he was gone again, like smoke lingering around my fingers. But this time, there was something different. Although my dad had gone, this time he had left his book behind. Picking up the copy of *Hamlet* and looking down at the page he had been reading, I noticed a smudge of blood across the page. It was like he had highlighted it for some reason. Wiping away my tears, I looked at the words beneath the crimson smear and it read, *'One may smile and smile, and be a villain!'* I laid the book back on the grass beneath the willow tree, just in case he came back for it.

Then, from a short distance away, I heard the sound of sobbing, but it wasn't the deep weeping sound that meandered on the breeze, it was something more. Standing, I pulled back the branches of the tree. There was another figure, this one smaller, slender in the distance and I knew at once who it was. I looked back once more at the book, but it had gone. There wasn't even a bent blade of grass to show that my dad had ever sat there against the tree.

Wiping the tears from my cheeks with the backs of my

hands, I headed through the trees towards Kayla. I didn't rush; I took my time, not wanting to intrude on her personal grief. Like the woods on the side of the Weeping Peak had brought my personal feelings of grief to the surface, they had also stirred something deep within Kayla.

As I approached her, I could see that she was standing before her own weeping willow, her face in her hands as she wept. Kayla's shoulders shuddered as she rocked back and forth, the sound of her sobbing blending with those that surrounded us. My first instinct was to go to her, hug her in my arms and to comfort her as much as I now needed to be comforted. But I held back, just on the other side of the branches that draped around her. Unseen by her, I peered through the leaves and watched her.

"I love you," she whispered, looking up as if talking to someone standing by the trunk of the tree. Turning my head so I could hear her over the sound of the weeping willows, I wondered who it was from her past that had visited her in these woods. Was it her father, Doctor Hunt? Or perhaps her mother, who had been murdered by Sparky?

"I know what I have to do," Kayla murmured. "I know the decision that Kiera has to make." Hearing Kayla mention my name, I snapped my head front and stared at her through the branches.

"I know that I have to be strong until the end," she continued as she looked ahead as if someone only she could see were standing before her.

From the snippets of her conversation I could hear over the sound of the continuous sobbing, I guessed it was her father she had found in the woods, just like I had found mine. I imagined that he was telling her that she had to be strong for me – after all, if the legend was to be believed, both Kayla and Isidor had been sent to help me.

Then I heard something, another voice, but it was lost amongst the rustling branches of the willows. Kayla continued to stare ahead at the trunk of the tree, tears spilling down her cheeks as her red hair billowed about her shoulders.

"I love you," she said again and buried her face in her

hands. I couldn't bear to see her suffering any longer, so pulling back the branches, I revealed myself to her. Snapping her head around, she glanced at me, then, quickly back at the tree. I went towards her, my arms open; and with thoughts of my own father in my head, tears began to roll from the corners of my eyes.

"Kayla, it's okay," I whispered as I folded my arms around her. But she never hugged me back, she felt rigid in my arms like a waxwork dummy. Then, looking over her shoulder at the tree, I could see a set of footprints in the grass where someone had been standing. Unlike my father's ghost, Kayla's had left a trail of footprints that disappeared back into the woods and out of sight.

"We should go," she said against my chest, as I continued to stare down at the tracks which had been left behind. Why hadn't I seen them? Because whoever Kayla had been talking to had been hidden from my view behind the trunk of the tree. She hadn't been looking at the tree at all – Kayla had been talking to someone who had been hiding behind it.

"Who were you talking to?" I whispered.

She made no reply. Then, pulling herself free of my grasp, she turned and headed back into the woods. I looked down at the footprints again and could see by the size that they belonged to a male. But there was something else; with my heart turning cold in my chest, I crouched down and picked up the discarded cigarette butt that had been left by the base of the tree.

Chapter Twenty

"Kayla!" I called after her, but she had gone. Not wanting to lose track of her in the woods, I flicked the cigarette butt away and raced after her.

Tearing aside the branches that blocked my path, I ran in the direction she had gone. At first I feared that I had lost her, then ahead I caught sight of her.

"Kayla!" I yelled. "Wait for me!"

She didn't stop, or even slow, so I raced after her. Reaching out, I took hold of her arm, spinning her around. "Kayla, are you all right?" I asked her.

"I guess," she said, looking at me, and I could see the tracks of tears running the length of her face.

"Why did you run away from me?" I asked her.

"Run away from you?" she said, looking confused.

"Back there," I said pointing back over my shoulder. "You were crying and I hugged you."

"Hugged me?" she asked, staring blankly at me. "You never hugged me."

"Yes, I did," I insisted.

"Kiera, we've been looking for you for ages," Kayla explained. "You went missing just after we entered the woods."

"But I was with you over there just a few moments ago," I breathed.

"Impossible," someone said, and I glanced back to see Luke and the others coming towards me.

"I know what I saw," I said. "You were by one of those weeping willows and you were crying."

"Not me," Kayla said and she did look genuinely puzzled.

"She's been with me the whole time," Luke added. "We've been looking for you."

"Kiera," Isidor said, coming close. "I told you these woods can play with your mind, your sanity." And he gently squeezed my shoulder.

"What else did you see, Kiera?" Luke asked, and his voice was soft and caring.

"My father," I said, now feeling utterly confused.

"But your father is dead," Luke whispered and touched my hand.

"It's these woods," Isidor insisted. "I told you we should never have come in here. I knew something like this would happen."

"Okay, Nostradamus," Potter growled, pushing Isidor aside. "Let's just get out of here."

"I agree," Luke said, taking me by the arm.

Pulling away from him, I snapped at them all, "I know what I saw!" Then turning, I stormed off through the weeping willows.

The others followed, and it was as if a dark blanket had fallen over all of us. It was more than just the oppressive atmosphere of the woods. There was a darkness seeping between us as a group – a group that had once been tight now seemed to be splitting apart, being unwound at the edges like a frayed rug. But why was this happening and who was yanking on the threads that were tearing us all apart?

Had I really seen Kayla? Had I really seen my father? Isidor had said that the woods messed with your head, that they were haunted by past feelings of sorrow that we had buried deep within us. But why hadn't the others been affected? I knew all of them were haunted by feelings of loss for loved ones. They had all been hurt. But why, then, had I seen Kayla? If she had just been a ghost, why had she been beneath that weeping willow? Kayla had never caused me any sorrow.

With my head feeling as if it had been wrung through a mangle, I saw the edge of the woods and hurried towards it, just wanting to be free of those weeping willows. Stepping back onto the side of the mountain, I could see that the light from the Light House had faded. The stalagmites which hung above me sparkled, and from where I stood, they did look like a sea of stars. How long had we been inside the woods? It was as if I had lost all sense of time. But how long did it take the Light House to turn? Did it rotate on a twenty-four hour cycle like the sun? I didn't know, and part of me didn't care. I just wanted to get to this Light House, get Kayla to hear whatever it was that Coanda hoped she might hear, and then...then what? Make our way to the Dust Palace and...decision time.

Pushing that thought from my mind, I stood and waited for the others to catch up. I watched them clear the edge of the woods and come towards me. They walked together and part of me felt left out, almost excluded from the group.

"It will be night soon," Coanda said as he strode towards me. Pointing ahead, he said, "We'll make camp just on the other side of that ridge."

Looking at Kayla, who was standing close to Potter, or was it the other way around? Was Potter standing close to Kayla? "What about this person who has been following us?" I asked.

"They've gone now," Kayla told me.

"How can you be so sure?" I asked her.

"Because I can't hear them," she half-smiled at me.

"Okay?" Coanda said, eyeing me.

"I'm fine," I told him, setting off towards the ridge where we were to make camp for the night.

The rest of the group hung back, as if sensing that I wanted – needed – to be alone. I scrambled over the ridge of rock and found myself in a circular clearing. The ground was rocky and uneven in places. The area was shielded by trees and I was relieved to not see one of those weeping willows, even though as the wind blew by, I was sure I could still hear them sobbing.

Walking to the outermost edge, I leant against a large rock and watched the others climb into the clearing. Potter glanced across at me and winked. Leaving the others, he came towards me.

"How you doing, tiger?" he whispered, popping a cigarette in the corner of his mouth.

"Just leave me alone," I told him.

"If you say you saw your dad in those woods, then I believe you," he said hunkering down beside me.

"And what about Kayla?" I hissed.

Shrugging his huge shoulders, he blew smoke from the corner of his mouth and said, "Did you really see her, Kiera?"

"I saw her!" I snapped and stared into his eyes.

Staring back into mine, Potter said, "Okay, I believe you."

"My dad was a ghost, I can accept that," I told him. "But Kayla wasn't. She was really there."

"Okay," he said. "I don't claim to understand why, but I believe you."

"Why?" I pushed.

Looking back over his shoulder at the others and then back at me he whispered, "Because I saw one or two of my own demons hiding out in those woods."

"Who?" I breathed.

"You wouldn't know him," Potter said.

"Who?" I insisted.

"A Lycanthrope," he told me, not meeting my gaze as if he felt ashamed in some way. "His name was Drake, and he paid the price for crimes he didn't commit."

"Why didn't you say this back in the woods?" I hissed. "Why did you let everyone think I was going mad?"

"Because I'm starting to believe that this Elias Munn wants you and everyone else to believe you're going mad. He wants us to question your judgment, Kiera – to stop people from having faith in you."

"And what about you?" I asked him. "Do you have faith in me, Potter?"

"Does a bear shit in the woods?" he smiled and winked at me. Then, without saying another word, he stood, dropped his smouldering cigarette butt, ground it out with the heel of his boot, and walked away. I sat and looked at that cigarette butt and recalled the one I had seen by the weeping willow. I continued to look at it while the others set up camp and the sky turned black.

Taking my iPod, I switched it on. Rolling onto my side and closing my eyes, I lay and listened to Will Young sing *Leave Right Now*, and I wished that I could.

Chapter Twenty-One

"She can't be!" The pathologist murmured as she hovered over me, scalpel only inches from my good eye.

"I'm alive in here!" I screamed inside my head. Got to get that scalpel away from me! Got to get that...

Then, without thought, more by instinct, I thrust out my hand and took hold of the pathologist's wrist. I curled the three fingers on my right hand with such force that the pathologist screamed, fearing her wrist bone would disintegrate.

"Get that thing away from me!" I yelled, but the words didn't sound anything like that. They came out sounding slushy, like water lapping against the side of a bath. My tongue rolled against the inside of my mouth and spittle sprayed from the small, circular opening where my lips had once been.

"Slet sat sing sway rom smeee!" I screamed again, jerking the pathologist's arm to the right and sending the scalpel flying across the lab. The guy with the needle ducked, then slipped backwards and crashed into a silver trolley that toppled over and sent surgical equipment clattering across the room.

The police officer backed away and began fumbling for his radio which was attached to his shirt. Groaning, the pathologist fell away, holding her wrist to her chest. I swung my legs over the edge of the mortuary slab and stood naked before them. My legs began to buckle in the middle and I staggered forward, leaning against the tiled wall of the mortuary to keep my balance.

"Slothes!" I screeched at them, holding out the two fingers that dangled from my left hand. "Slothes!"

"What?" the Pathologist mumbled, her face as white as her medical coat.

"Slothes!" I said again, through the hole in my face.

"She wants her clothes," the police officer said, stepping away from the wall on the opposite side of the mortuary. I looked at him with my one bloodshot eye and nodded in agreement. "Slothes," I said again, holding out what was left of my hands. "Slothes spleese."

"Give the girl her clothes," the officer ordered to the lab assistant.

I watched as the assistant gathered my clothes from a nearby workbench. Everything appeared to be in infrared. The assistant came towards me like a child nearing a dog that had a history of biting. When he was within a few feet of me, the lab assistant chucked the clothes in a ball at my feet.

Bending, I picked up the black overalls and threaded one of my legs into them. Lurching from side to side, I looked at the lab assistant and shouted, "Selp smee!"

The assistant looked at me, trying to decipher what it was that I wanted.

"Help her put her clothes on," the officer said as he tried to remove his radio from his shirt hoping he hadn't drawn my attention to what he was planning to do.

Coming forward, the assistant bent down and pulled the legs of the overalls up to my waist. I leant against him for support and the assistant shuddered under my icy touch and...

Chapter Twenty-Two

...I was woken by the sound of screaming. Sitting bolt upright, I could already see that Potter was on his feet and staring into the trees that surrounded the camp. Luke jumped up, followed by Coanda, but where were Isidor and Kayla? And who had been screaming?

Tucking my iPod away, I raced into the centre of the camp. The fire that had been made was now nothing more than a pile of smouldering ash. It was still night and those stalagmites continued twinkle above us.

"Who was screaming?" I asked the others, but before any of them had a chance to answer, Isidor came staggering from amongst the trees and into the camp. His hands were held out before him and something black dripped from them. He made a gasping sound in the back of his throat, as if he were having difficulty in breathing. He looked down at his hands, his mouth open.

"Isidor?" I yelled as I raced towards him. "What's happened?"

As if in answer to my question, he held his hands up and I could see they were covered in blood. "Isidor, have you hurt yourself?" I asked, feeling my own panic start to rise inside of me.

Staring at me from between his bright red fingers, he shook his head and mumbled, "Kayla."

"Kayla!" I snapped at him, fighting the urge to shake some sense into him. "Where's Kayla? What has happened to her?"

Then, turning slowly, he pointed one blood-soaked finger back towards the trees and I watched as it dripped with red stuff. Realising I wouldn't get any sense from him, I brushed him aside and ran towards the trees. Screwing up my eyes, I stared into the slices of blackness between the trees. I could see where they had been broken down and bent aside where Isidor had made his way towards them. Following the tracks he had left behind, I raced amongst the trees.

"Kayla!" I hollered. "Kayla where are you?"

I could hear the others come floundering through the trees behind me, and I cursed them under my breath as I feared that they could well be destroying any tracks that might have been left behind. But I didn't have time to give them a lecture in crime scene preservation right now, so I pushed on. Then just ahead, I could see something that made my heart stop. My fears of there being a crime scene were correct as I spied Kayla lying dead on the ground just feet from me. I stood rooted to the spot and looked down at her. Kayla lay on her back, her arms splayed out on either side of her. Her eyes were open and blank-looking. Her hands were curled into fists and her head looked misshapen and covered in blood. Her thick, red hair lay in bloody stripes across her face where it had stuck to the blood. The urge was to run to her and cradle her in my arms, but I had to bury my feelings deep inside me. If I ever had to keep control, it was now. I wouldn't do Kayla any justice if I raced forward and destroyed any clues that might have been left. I would catch whomever had done this to her and rip their fucking heart out. So fighting back my own tears, I looked over my shoulder at Luke, Potter, and Coanda who raced towards me.

"Stop!" I ordered, showing them the flat of my hand. "Don't come any closer."

"What's going on here?" Coanda barked. Then, peering over my shoulder and looking down at Kayla's corpse, he whispered, "Oh for fuck's sake!" But he didn't say it as if he was upset by the death of my friend, he sounded annoyed that it was going to hamper with what he had planned at the Light House.

Luke and Potter joined us and seeing Kayla spread dead before them, Luke turned away and Potter just froze, his eyes fixed firmly on the sight before him.

"Who did this?" I heard Luke whisper. "She was just a child."

"That's what I want to find out," I whispered back, fighting the urge to cry.

Potter made a move towards her body. Taking him by the arm, I looked up into his face and said, "She's dead, Potter. If you want to help her, stand back and just let me…just let me *see*. Okay?"

Swallowing hard, he looked at me and nodded.

Turning, I hunkered down and taking a deep breath, I ran my fingers over the surface of the ground around Kayla's body. Screwing up my eyes so I could penetrate the darkness, I searched the area. Moving forward inch by inch, I let my eyes wander over the crime scene. When I was happy I had seen everything, I turned my attention to Kayla. Taking hold of her feet, I lifted them gently and let my fingers dance over her boot laces. I ran my fingers up the length of her overalls. At the neck, I unzipped them. Folding back the material to reveal her chest, I winced at the sight of the gaping wound and bite marks just above her right nipple. I placed my fingertips on the inside of her clothes, letting my fingers brush over the material. Once I was satisfied, I turned to her hands. I uncurled her fingers and gasped. In each palm she clutched a severed ear. Looking briefly at her fingernails, I then held my breath and gently brushed away the hair that covered her face. As I feared, both of her ears had been bitten off and it was those which she clutched in her fists.

Closing her eyelids, I heard Potter say "Well?"

Standing, I looked at them and could see that Isidor had worked his way back through the trees and was cowering just behind Coanda.

"What did you see, Kiera?" Luke asked, his eyes wide.

"Kayla was murdered by two people. One male, the other female. She came out here to meet them as if it had already been planned," I started. "She knew them well. She took her clothes off for them, why, I'm not sure, but she definitely removed her clothes. She didn't put up a fight so it's as if she knew she was coming out here to die. A sacrifice, perhaps?"

"How can you be so sure of this?" Coanda asked. "How do you know there were two killers? And that she removed her clothes? Look, she's wearing them!"

"She's wearing her clothes now. But at the time of her death she was naked," I started to explain, crouching over Kayla's dead body again. "Look at her bootlaces. These weren't tied by Kayla, they were tied by someone else."

"Don't tell me your gift is so powerful that you can see finger prints on a piece of string in the dark," Coanda scoffed. "It's way easier than that," I said, not bothering to look at him. "Anyone can see this stuff if only you took the time to look. If Kayla had tied them herself, the first loop in the laces would be facing the inside of the boot, but these don't show that. The loop faces the outside of the shoe; therefore, they had been re-tied by someone else as they stood over her. She had to be naked at the time of death as her heart has been ripped out and that causes a fountain of blood. But the thing is, there is no blood down the front of her boiler suit, but plenty on her chest and down the front of her body. Again, this suggests that she was redressed once she was dead."

"So how do you know that she knew these people and had planned to meet them out here?" Coanda asked, still sounding unconvinced by what I was telling him.

"Would you take your clothes off for just anyone?" I asked, cocking an eyebrow at him. "Knowing Kayla like I did, she would have put up a fight and I've seen Kayla in too many fights to know that she attacks with her claws first. There are no signs of flesh or blood under her fingernails. No, she didn't fight back, she got undressed willingly. If she had come out here for any other reason than to meet somebody, she wouldn't be dead now. Let's just say she woke up and needed to pee, so she came out here. She would have heard them creeping up on her. As you know, Coanda, she had an amazing sense of hearing. As soon as she knew someone was close, she would have fled or stood her ground and attacked. But as we can see, she did neither of those things."

"But you said something about a sacrifice?" Luke quizzed me, and I could see that all the colour had drained from his face in shock.

"Even when she was having her heart eaten from her chest, Kayla still didn't fight back," I said. "Apart from her clean fingernails, there are no signs of a struggle in the area; and besides, we weren't that far away, we would have heard it. You try and eat somebody's heart out of their chest and bite their ears off, they will put up a fight."

"They bit her ears off?" Coanda breathed, and behind him, Isidor threw up.

"Yes," I said, trying to keep my own emotions under wrap.

"Why would they have bitten her ears off?" Potter asked, his face grim-looking and hard, as if chipped from stone.

"There was something the killers didn't want her to hear, I guess," I shuddered.

"Hear what?" Luke asked looking at me.

But before I could say anything, Coanda came towards me with a look of realisation on his face. "They knew where we were heading, that's why they killed her. They knew we wanted her to listen," he said in disbelief.

"Listen to what?" Luke snapped impatiently.

Then gripping me by the arms, our noses almost touching, Coanda hissed, "Only you and I knew where we were heading, Kiera. I told you not to tell anyone. Didn't I tell you that her life would be put in danger, that Munn would try and stop her from ever reaching the Light House?"

"Light House?" Luke muttered. "What are you going on about? I thought we were heading for the Dust Palace."

Ignoring Luke, Coanda shook me by the shoulders and roared into my face, "Who did you tell, Kiera? Who did you tell that we were heading for the Light House and what Kayla was going to do once we got there?"

There was only one person I had confided in, and looking over Coanda's shoulder, my heart sank to see that Potter had now vanished.

Chapter Twenty-Three

"What's going on here?" Luke asked. "And where has Potter gone?"

Hearing this, Coanda gripped my shoulder and barked, "You told him, didn't you!"

Yes I had told Potter, but I trusted him. He would never have hurt Kayla. He wasn't part of this. I glanced over at Isidor, who stood looking at me, his hands still wet with his sister's blood. His eyes were dark, the rings beneath them looking like two half-moons.

I broke his stare and looking at Coanda, I snapped, "Potter isn't a part of this!"

"How can you be so sure?" Coanda roared and I could see the anger in his eyes.

"I asked him if he were Elias Munn and he said he wasn't," I told him.

"Oh well that makes everything all right then," Coanda sneered. "Are you freaking stupid or what? Do you honestly think he would admit to something like that when we are so close to the Dust Palace? He's lied to you!"

"He wouldn't lie to me!" I snapped back at him.

"And what makes you so sure about that?" Coanda seethed, and he stared at me so intently that his icy blue eyes seemed to penetrate my very soul.

"Because he loves me," I whispered, lowering my head.

"What did you say?" Luke asked, stepping forward.

"Potter is in love with me," I said, but couldn't bring myself to look at him.

"He loves you?" Luke murmured, sounding lost and confused. "Since when?"

Raising my head, I looked into his eyes and said, "I'm in love with Potter, I'm sorry Luke." To see the expression on his face broke my heart. He looked as if someone had snuck up on him and punched him in the guts. "I'm so sorry," I whispered and reached for him.

Knocking my hand away, he said, "This can't be true.

You're just saying this to cover the fact that you've told him this secret you and Coanda were keeping from us. You don't know what you're saying."

"Luke, I do know what I'm saying," I told him softly. "I love Potter."

"But why?" he asked in disbelief.

"Why not?" I said back.

"Where do you want me to start?" he snapped and I could see his hurt turning into frustration. "Isn't the fact that he's Potter reason enough?"

"The same Potter who risked his life to rescue you from the zoo?" I said, trying to hide my rising frustration with Luke. "The same Potter who has risked his life on countless occasions to save all of us? Why shouldn't I fall in love with someone like that?"

With an exasperated look on his face, Luke said, "But I thought we...you know...I thought there was something between us. And I've saved you too, Kiera."

I thought of how Luke had risked his life back at The Ragged Cove, how he had dived into the burning church and countless other times, but I didn't want to get into an argument about who had been the most gallant. I couldn't help the way I felt about Potter. Why do we fall in love with anyone? Do any of us really know the answer to that?

"I know you saved me too, Luke," I told him. "But Potter..."

"Is arrogant, offensive, violent...do I need to go on?" Coanda cut in.

Looking at the both of them, I said, "I *see* more than that in him. I see through all of that."

Then as if from nowhere, Isidor brushed past us and said, "If you don't mind, I'm gonna go and bury my sister while you stand and bicker about your love lives."

"Hey Isidor," I said, trying to take his arm. "I'm sorry, you're right. We'll help."

"Don't bother," he said coldly, kneeling down and gently scooping Kayla up into his arms.

"Isidor," I said softly, but he ignored me and all I could do was watch helplessly as he carried his sister away amongst the trees.

"I'm going back to the camp," Coanda said, shaking his head, not in sorrow but frustration that his plan had now been thwarted.

Luke and I stood and looked at each other and the silence was louder than any sound. When I thought I couldn't bear it any longer, Luke said, "And what if Potter really is this Elias Munn, are you going to still love him then?"

"He's not Elias Munn," I insisted.

"Potter got you to fall in love with him, which is what Munn has wanted the whole time," Luke said. "He got you to tell him about Coanda's plan. Kayla's dead and Potter has disappeared. Can't you see that, Kiera? I thought you could *see* things."

Luke's words went around and around in my head and I thought of the letter that Ravenwood had left for me.

'Elias Munn plunged his fist into her chest and tore her heart out, screaming that if he couldn't have her heart than no other man could.'

Again those images of Potter tearing Eloisa's heart from her chest came back to haunt me. The woman Elias Munn had killed, had she really been this Sophie that Potter had told me about? The girl he had fallen in love with – his first love? After all, I only had Potter's word that he flew from her bedroom window that night – leaving her alive and in tears at the realisation he was a Vampyrus. Could Sophie be the woman Ravenwood referred to in his letter to me?

Staring at Luke, I said, "Can you honestly say you believe Potter is Elias Munn?"

"I don't know what to believe anymore," he said, shaking his head. "I believed Potter and I were friends. I thought we were like brothers. What sort of brother would go after the woman I had fallen in love with? Tell me that, Kiera. What sort of friend is Potter when he does something like that to me?"

"But it wasn't just Potter," I tried to explain. "It was me too."

"I don't believe that," Luke said. "Potter has seduced you – tricked you like he has tricked me. He's tricked all of us. I thought I could trust him, but while I was imprisoned, which only happened so I could save your life, Kiera, he went behind my back and stole you from me."

"I'm not some kind of prize, you know," my frustration starting to boil beneath the surface. "Potter didn't steal me from anyone – I knew what I was doing. I couldn't help the feelings I had for him."

"So that's it then?" Luke said, and again his eyes were awash with that look of hurt. "It's you and Potter."

"I do care about you Luke, honestly I do," I said, I wasn't trying to soften the blow; I did really care for him.

"You have a funny way of showing it," he snapped, then at once he shook his head, and added, "I'm sorry, Kiera, I didn't mean that. I'm just hurting you know. I've lost you and my best friend in the space of a few minutes."

"You haven't lost me," I told him. "I'm your friend."

"But friendship isn't enough for me, Kiera, I'm in love with you," he said.

"Please, Luke, don't say that," I whispered.

"But it's true."

"I'm sorry."

"So am I," he whispered, turning and heading back towards camp.

I stood alone in the woods and felt totally and utterly lost. Covering my face with my hands, I started to sob. What had I done? Had I really been tricked by Potter? Had I really been responsible for the death of Kayla by telling him Coanda's plan? Why had he disappeared when Coanda realised I hadn't kept his confidence? There were so many questions and I hated myself. Not because of what I had done, but because I just couldn't see. All my life I had been able to see what others had missed – the finer details – but now when I needed to the most, I couldn't see anything, it was like I was blind.

I couldn't believe that Potter had deceived me. But was that just me trying to convince myself I was too smart to be deceived by him? Was it my pride and own arrogance getting in the way? Was that what was blinding me?

But still there was something deep down that told me

Potter was not part of this. It was something very small, but big enough for me to grab onto. All I could see in my mind's eye was that cigarette butt left by the weeping willow in the woods. And it was that single cigarette butt which kept me hoping that Potter wasn't Elias Munn.

Chapter Twenty-Four

There was a sound behind me and I spun round to see Isidor coming back through the trees into the clearing. I could see that he had been crying, and he cuffed away a stream of snot from beneath his nose with his sleeve. Wiping my own tears away, I went towards him, but before I got to him, he raised a hand indicating for me not to come too close.

"I'm so sorry, Isidor," I said.

He stood and stared at me and he had that haunted look again, the one he'd had since returning to The Hollows.

"What's wrong, Isidor?" I whispered.

"What do you think is wrong?" he came back at me. "My sister has just been murdered."

"But there's something more than that," I told him. "You've not been right since we got here. Please talk to me, Isidor." Again, I tried to move closer to him, but he stepped backwards, maintaining the gap between us.

"Whatever's wrong, Isidor, you're going to have to talk about it sooner or later," I said. "Keeping it to yourself won't help."

Lowering his head so I couldn't see into his eyes, he said, "It's Kayla..." then stopped.

"What about Kayla?" I asked him.

Straightening up, he looked at me and said, "It's nothing." Then, he was gone, slowly walking back to camp with his crossbow slung over his shoulder.

Alone again, I peered back into the dark in the direction Isidor had come. I wanted to say my own goodbye to Kayla. I couldn't just leave her lying alone on the side of the mountain. So, following Isidor's tracks back through the trees, I came across a mound of disturbed earth. Kneeling beside it, I ran my fingertips over the dirt and it was hard for me to accept that she lay just beneath my touch, battered and bruised, heart and ears missing. How had it come to this? This wasn't the way her life should have ended. Kayla deserved better than that. I remembered the time I'd watched her giggling in the dark at

Hallowed Manor as she taught herself to fly, and tears began to roll down my cheeks.

"I'll miss you, Kayla," I said.

Then I felt a hand fall on my shoulder. Stifling a scream, I looked up to see Potter standing behind me. I jumped up, and within an instant my claws were out, as were my fangs, and I launched him across the small clearing. Potter flew backwards under the weight of my punch and slammed into the trunk of a large tree. It shook in the ground and leaves showered down from above. Before he'd had the chance to regain his composure, I was on him, my claws around his throat, my fangs inches from his face.

"Did you kill her?" I screeched.

"No!" he groaned beneath my grip.

"Why did you run?"

"Because I'm being set up," he wheezed.

"By who?"

"I don't know."

"How do I know you're not lying to me?" I spat, spittle spraying from my fangs and covering his face.

"You don't, but you'll have to trust me," he croaked.

"Who did you tell about the Light House?"

"No one, Kiera."

"So if only three of us knew about it, one of us is the killer and I know it isn't me," I hissed.

"Do you really believe I killed Kayla?" Potter mumbled, and I could see his lips were turning blue.

In my heart I didn't believe he had murdered Kayla; so slowly, I released my grip on him. I looked at him as he rubbed his throat and prayed I had done the right thing by letting him go. Stepping away, I went back towards Kayla's grave.

"I didn't kill Kayla," Potter said joining me, his voice still sounding raw from where I had strangled him. "But somebody wants you to believe I did."

"Who?" I asked, not looking at him.

"Elias Munn."

"And who is he?"

"Someone close to us," he said. "I didn't think I would ever say this, but I think Murphy was right, someone in our group is a traitor."

"So what's changed your mind?"

"Being framed for Kayla's murder is probably a good start," he said, taking a cigarette from his pocket and lighting it. Then looking through the cloud of blue smoke at me, he added, "You don't look too surprised by the whole idea of me being framed."

"Put the cigarette out," I ordered him.

"What?" he said, looking bemused. "I've only just lit it."

"Put the goddamn thing out, Potter!"

Without taking his eyes off me, he took the smouldering cigarette from the corner of his mouth, dropped it onto the grass, and ground it out with the heel of his boot.

Staring down at it, I asked, "What do you see?"

"A waste of a perfectly good smoke," Potter grimaced.

"Tell me what you see," I pushed.

"You're doing that Miss Marple thing again, aren't you?" he sighed.

Ignoring him, I knelt down and ran my fingertips over the cigarette and the blades of grass. In my head I could see the cigarette left by the tree where Kayla had been crying. I compared the two images in my mind. "Come here," I told him.

Sighing, Potter knelt beside me.

I picked up the cigarette butt and held it up to him. "It's crushed to pieces."

"Even I can see that," he said.

"Just like the other one," I whispered.

"What other one?" he asked me.

"The one by the weeping willow," I breathed. "But there is a difference."

"What are you talking about?" he asked, gripping me by the shoulder.

"There was a cigarette left by the weeping willow where I discovered Kayla crying. She had been talking to someone. At first I thought it was the ghost of her father, just like mine had visited me. But when I went to her, I could see that it hadn't been a ghost at all, but a living person, as I could see their footprints in the grass as if they had run away. Whoever had been standing there left one of your cigarette ends. Knowing I would see it, they hoped I would think it was you she had been talking to."

"So what makes you think that it wasn't me?" he asked.

"The cigarette had been ground out beneath the heel of your boot, because it was crushed just like this one," I told him holding up what was left of the cigarette. But look at the grass. See how it is all bent over and disturbed where you ground it out with the heel of your boot? Well, the grass beneath the willow wasn't. The cigarette hadn't been put out there; it had been planted by whoever wanted to frame you. But by who, I don't know."

Standing, Potter looked at me and said, "And whoever put it there killed Kayla. Somehow they knew you had confided in me about the detour to the Light House, so they planted the cigarette and then killed Kayla hoping you would put the facts together and would suspect me."

"But there was only one other person that knew that we were heading for the Light House," I told him. "And that was Coanda. Why would he kill Kayla when it was his idea to take her there in the first place?"

"What about Isidor?" Potter asked. "I've always thought that guy was a bit weird."

"Isidor?" I breathed. "Never."

"That's just what I don't get," Potter said. "There's been something wrong with the guy ever since we got here. He's been moody and distant – he's hardly said two words to anyone. Isidor is the one who found Kayla's body. He was the one who came staggering from the woods smothered in Kayla's blood and no one suspects a thing? It's like the kid is fireproof or something!"

"But he wouldn't have murdered Kayla," I said.

"Neither would I," Potter said razor quick. "But that hasn't stopped everyone from pointing the finger at me. I wasn't the one sniffing her dead body."

"What do you mean?"

"I watched Isidor bury Kayla from the shelter of the trees,"

Potter explained. "At first I thought he was kissing her goodbye or something, but then I realised he was sniffing her dead body. Now why would he go and do a thing like that?"

"I don't know," I said thoughtfully.

"Whatever the reason," Potter said, "There's something wrong with that kid."

"I still don't think he murdered Kayla," I told him.

"Someone did and it wasn't me," Potter insisted.

"I believe you," I said, looking at him. "But what are you going to do now?"

"Hang back," he explained. "I'm going to follow you from a distance. This Elias Munn, whoever he might be, is close and I reckon he wants to get to the Dust Palace as much as you do."

"I thought you didn't believe in him – just like Father Christmas," I reminded him.

"Being framed for a murder you didn't commit gives you a different perspective on things," he said. "Now you go and I'll watch your back, I won't be far away. I'll follow you to the Dust Palace, that's where I think this Elias Munn will reveal himself to you."

"And what happens if he does?"

"Then we finish it," Potter said. "We finish him."

"And then what?" I asked, taking Potter's hands in mine.

"What do you mean?"

"Will we get some time together?" I asked, looking up into his black eyes. "What I mean is, we have spent our whole time on the run so far. It would be so nice to…you know…go on a proper date or something. I'd like to get to know you, for you to get to know me. All I really know about you is that you have a tendency for *WHAM* songs! I don't know what your favourite food is, your favourite movie…I don't know anything about you."

Taking my face gently in his huge hands, Potter leant close and said, "I'd love to go on a date with you, Kiera Hudson, but for that to happen you're gonna have to choose the Vampyrus over the humans, because if you don't, I'm dead."

Then, before I had the chance to say anything, he kissed me softly on the mouth, stepped into the shadows beneath the trees and was gone.

Chapter Twenty-Five

The others were waiting for me by the burnt out embers of the fire. It was still dark, the Light House had yet to complete its circuit for the night. The embers smouldered angrily and a thin line of smoke trailed up amongst the stalagmites.

Luke glanced at me as I re-entered the camp, then looked quickly away. Isidor stood, ashen-faced and tired-looking, his crossbow in his hands. He fixed me with a stare, but unlike Luke had done, he didn't look away.

"You took your time," Coanda grumbled at me, eager to get going. "What were you doing back there?"

"Saying goodbye to Kayla," I said, and I couldn't bring myself to look at Isidor.

"Let's get going," he said, turning as if to leave the camp.

"Go where?" Isidor asked him.

"To the Light House," Coanda said as if it should've been blatantly obvious to him.

"What's the point?" Luke asked. "Kayla's dead. The mission has changed. I think we should head straight for the Dust Palace."

"No," Coanda shot back at him. "Elias Munn has agents there ready to send out his signal. Kayla might not be with us anymore, and you're right, the mission has changed, but if we can't intercept the messages, then we will kill those who are planning to send it."

"I think Luke is right," I cut in. "Potter told me that going to the Light House was suicide."

"And when exactly did he tell you these words of wisdom?" Coanda sneered, his clear blue eyes clouded with distrust.

"When I told him about your plan," I explained. "He said -"

"I'm not interested in anything he had to say," Coanda barked at me. "Potter's not to be trusted."

"But if Potter is Elias Munn, or some kind of traitor like you believe him to be," I snapped back, "Then won't he be expecting us to head for the Light House?"

"Not without Kayla," Coanda went on. "He wouldn't believe

we have the balls to go and attack his agents there. He'd expect us to go running to the Elders with our tails between our legs. But that ain't my style, Hudson. I don't shy away from a fight."

"So I've heard," I muttered.

"What did you say?" Coanda asked, jutting his chin in my direction.

"Nothing," I said back.

"Then let's get going," he growled, turning his back on me and marching away from the camp.

With his head bowed forward, Isidor slowly set off after him. Luke was next to leave the camp. "So you are just going to go along with him?" I asked Luke.

Ignoring me, he continued after Coanda. I trotted after him, and taking Luke by the arm, I said, "How do we know we can trust Coanda? He could be leading us into a trap."

Luke prised my fingers from his arm, and looking at me he said, "I thought I could trust you and Potter once, now I don't know who to trust anymore."

"Luke," I breathed, not sure what to say next.

But before I'd had the chance to say anything, Luke said, "Kiera, do me a favour and leave me alone for a while."

I watched him walk away, his shoulders slumped forward, and I hated myself for hurting him. But I couldn't take it back now, even if I wanted to and I wasn't sure that I did. I disliked myself even more for feeling that way.

The four of us walked through the night in silence. We reached the top of the mountain where it flattened out into a hard-panned surface. It was so hard and arid that it was covered in deep groves and cracks. Just like the ground Potter and I had raced over to reach the canyon, the ground was an orange-red colour and was covered in a fine ash. Did it ever rain here? I wondered. And I doubted that it did. But nothing would have surprised me about The Hollows or so I thought.

Just as I began to consider the possibility of rain falling in this new world I had fallen into, it started to snow. I stared, mesmerised up into the dark as giant white flakes began to seesaw down towards me. They covered the ground ahead, laying a white carpet before us.

"Snow?" I gasped in wonder.

"Ash!" Coanda grunted.

"Ash?"

"We're nearing the Light House," Coanda said, and it was as if his voice had taken on a tone of reverence. "The lake of lava that it floats on blisters and bubbles at such temperatures that almost everything it touches burns, sending up clouds of ash."

"Almost everything?" I asked him.

"Except the Light House," he said. "No one knows why it hasn't eroded into the lake – no one truly understands its power."

"Look at that," Isidor said, short of breath, pointing into the distance.

I looked in the direction he was pointing and drew a deep breath. The horizon glowed – in fact it pulsated like a sunrise seeping from the ground. The sky in front of us burnt crimson, pink, and gold. The light splayed across the night like electric fingers. Ash flew up into the air like giant flakes of glistening ticker tape. But the light rose quicker and brighter than any sunrise I had ever seen.

With my forearm across my eyes, I said to Coanda, "Where has the light come from so quickly?"

"We're close to the Light House and it's turning towards us," he seemed to roar in excitement and awe. "C'mon, we don't have time to admire its beauty!" And he was off, racing across the hard-panned ground towards the light.

Without question, we followed him. As we grew near, I noticed what looked like a black splinter running the length of the light. With my eyes almost shutting against the glare and my skin starting to prickle with heat, I could see that it wasn't a crack in the light at all, but the Light House. Just as Potter had described it to me, the Light House was a needle of rock that towered out of the Earth's core and up into the night. It was narrow and wizened-looking, like a decrepit spine that had had its flesh picked from it.

As we drew nearer, the light grew brighter, and the heat more intense. My skin prickled and beads of sweat rolled from my forehead and onto my cheeks. The ground before me shimmered with heat rays and the horizon looked as if it were bending back and forth, melting in front of my very eyes. Bending forward, we ploughed through the falling ash, which was now knee-deep and hot to the touch. It sparkled like the burning embers of a fire. We walked in a line, Luke to my right, Isidor and Coanda to my left. Then, the night or was it now day, was filled with a crackling, hissing, and spitting sounds. Raising one of his bony hands into the air, Coanda ordered us to stop. "This is as far as we go." He looked down at his feet which were covered in ash, and I almost screamed.

Before me was an abyss. It ran away from us into the distance like a river of seething sunlight. Covering my eyes, I peered down through my fingers as the lava sloshed in giant waves against the foot of the Light House. They crashed against the rocks, spraying up plumes of fiery surf.

I looked to my right at Luke and his face glowed red from the glare of the seething lake below and in that moment he looked like a god. His finely chiselled face, green eyes and that black hair that always fell across his brow reminded me of what had originally attracted me to him. As if sensing that I was looking at him, he turned to face me, and instead of glaring at me like I feared he would, he gave me the warmest of smiles and said, "It's incredible isn't it?"

"It's beautiful," I whispered back.

"But they're not so beautiful," someone said from behind me.

I looked back to find Coanda staring up at the jagged tip of the Light House. Peering through the light, I could see a swarm of Vampyrus circling. Their wings were spread and they looked as if they were protecting the Light House, defending it until they were summoned to send out the order to attack.

"The Light House will soon have turned our way and we will be seen," Coanda said. "We find shelter from its heat today, and make our move tonight." Then he was striding away towards a wide crack in the ground that zigzagged away from us like a giant wound.

I looked at Luke and Isidor who, without saying a word, followed Coanda as he climbed down into the fracture in the ground. Before following them, I looked back over my shoulder, scanning the horizon and hoping I would see Potter. But he was nowhere to be seen. So turning away, I climbed into the crack.

Chapter Twenty-Six

The fracture in the ground was deep, and by the time I had levered myself over the edge, the others were already at the bottom. The sides of the crack were made of hard, red rock and were warm to the touch. With care, I lowered myself to the bottom, finding myself in something not too dissimilar to a cave. It stretched away for as far as the eyes could see in both directions, becoming narrower and narrower.

The area we now stood in was open and vast. The rock above me formed a lip, which Coanda climbed beneath. We followed, only to find ourselves in a compact alcove. Coanda pulled a flashlight from one of the many pockets that adorned his overalls. He switched it on and cast a cone of bright white light across the walls. No sooner had the light splashed across them, then they began to glow a luminous green. I could see the walls were covered with that seaweed-type plant I had seen in the tunnel when first crawling into The Hollows.

The seaweed, if that's what it was, sent a sickly glow across the alcove, painting our faces the colour of Halloween masks. I glanced at Luke and he no longer looked like a god, but sallow and sick, as if just getting over some prolonged illness. I looked at Isidor and Coanda, and they too looked ill. Isidor removed his rucksack and crossbow, placing them on the ground and sighing as he arched his back. In the distance I could hear the sound of water dripping, and to think that there might be water in such an arid place seemed strange to me. The sound of it made me realise how thirsty I was, and my throat felt as if it had been coated in a layer of dust.

"How come I hear water?" I asked Coanda.

"Why is that so strange?" he shot back.

"It's just that this place, up above, seems so dry," I said.

"Come with me and I'll show you something," he said turning away and walking to the furthest reaches of the alcove. I foilowed him, Isidor and Luke trailing at my heels. When I thought Coanda was going to walk straight into the wall, he turned sharply to his left and squeezed himself through a narrow gap. Drawing breath, I snuck through the gap and stepped out onto a ledge. Luke and Isidor joined me, but neither of them looked upon the sight with the same amount of awe I did. Perhaps they had seen it all before, but the vines that hung from the ceiling were beautiful in this cave I now found myself in. The ledge ran along the side of what looked like a giant bowl, and from above hung an intricate weave of vines and roots, like those of a giant tree. They curled and wrapped themselves about one another like the most carefully platted length of hair. The roots and vines glowed green just like the seaweed-type plant that covered the walls in the alcove. They glistened wetly with a yellow liquid which dripped from them like some kind of honey.

Coanda knelt on the ledge. Steadying himself with one hand, he reached into the vast bowl with his other hand and dipped his fingers into the gloopy liquid which had collected there. He pulled his hand free and held it up before me, his eyes gleaming in the yellow light that the substance was omitting. Then, without taking his eyes off mine, he ran his tongue up the length of his fingers as if savouring a lollipop. The goo ran from his lips and it looked sticky and wet as if he had just gone berserk with a bottle of lip gloss.

Once he had licked his fingers clean, and with a look of sheer delight on his face, he smacked his lips together and said, "Root Juice - there's nothing like it."

Without hesitating further, both Luke and Isidor were on their hands and knees, reaching down and taking a fist full of the yellow goo. Holding their hands to their mouths, they slurped and sucked the liquid from between their fingers.

"Go on, Kiera," Coanda said, and it was the first time on our journey I had seen him smile – well, half-smile if I am to be honest.

"It doesn't look as if it will quench my thirst," I said, watching it drip in thick steams from Luke's fingers. "It looks kinda sticky."

"Just try it," Coanda urged.

With my throat in need of any kind of moisture, I knelt down and tenderly dipped my fingers into the liquid that dripped from the roots sprouting from the rocky ceiling. It felt warm, and just as I had suspected, very sticky. Gingerly, I raised my fingers to my mouth and closing my eyes, I prodded the liquid with my tongue. At once my whole body tingled, as if it had just drank from a mountain spring. Although it had felt warm to the touch, it felt ice cold against my tongue. Sticking my fingers into my mouth I sucked the Root Juice from them. The inside of my mouth seemed to explode to life as the sticky substance ran down my throat. At once, my thirst was quenched and I could never imagine myself feeling thirsty ever again. But it wasn't just the icy cold, mouth-watering sensation, it was the taste. It was as sweet as honey but sharp as a lemon, and I wanted more.

I licked my fingers clean and reached into the giant bowl again. Before my fingers even touched the goo, Coanda gripped me by the shoulder and pulled me back from the edge.

"No more, Kiera," he said, as if in warning.

"Why not?" I asked him, trying to hide my disappointment. "It's wonderful."

"In small amounts," Luke cut in. "Too much of the stuff can make you go crazy and you'll just want more and more."

"What's wrong with that?" I asked. "It tastes amazing."

"Just enough will kill your thirst," Coanda said. "But any more and it will kill you."

"What, like poison?" I gasped, wishing now I hadn't tried it, however nice it had been.

"It will drown you," Luke told me.

"Drown me?"

"How quickly did it cure your thirst?" he asked, staring at me.

"With just one drop."

"Just imagine, then, what a handful, or a bottleful of the stuff would do," Luke continued. "No one knows why, but the Root Juice retains water, that's how plants and trees survive in The Hollows. A cup full of the stuff will keep a tree watered for months. So when it reaches your stomach it turns to a water-like substance. And you'll just want more and more, and even when your stomach is bloated full and your bladder is screaming to be emptied, you'll want to carry on drinking and drinking until there isn't any more room in your stomach. Your lungs will start to fill and even when you are gasping for air, you'll be slurping up that wonderful-tasting Root Juice until you suffocate - until it smothers you."

"You won't need water for hours now, maybe even a day or two," Coanda said, and patted his flat stomach as if he himself were content. "The small amount you had will be enough to keep you hydrated just like it does the trees and the plants in The Hollows." Then, without saying another word on the matter, Coanda slipped back into the narrow gap and was gone.

I looked over at the roots that hung from the roof of the cave, watching the gloopy Root Juice dripping from them.

"Don't be tempted, Kiera," Luke said, then he too disappeared, leaving Isidor and me alone.

Isidor stood on the ledge and looked down into the hollow of the cave and at the goo laying there. He had that haunted look in his eyes and I took the opportunity of being alone to speak with him.

"Neat stuff, huh?" I started.

"I guess," he said back, but his voice sounded dreamy as if coming from a long way off.

Standing next to him, so close that my arm brushed against his, I said, "You never told me that you came from such an amazing world."

"You never asked," he replied thoughtfully.

Then, resting my hand on his arm, I said, "Please talk to me, Isidor. I know you are hurting about Kayla. I am too. We could help each other."

"I don't need any help," he said, but not in anger or in resentment, but with a tinge of sorrow.

"I'll find out who murdered Kayla," I promised him. "I know how much you had grown to love her, Isidor, and I loved her too. You were her brother but she was like a sister -"

"Somebody else loved her," Isidor suddenly said.

"Sorry? What did you say?"

"Someone else loved her," he said again. "Or they told her they did."

"Who are you talking about?" I quizzed, now feeling totally confused.

"She believed him," Isidor said, "In her own way, she looked up to him, admired him, wanted to be like him. So when he told her she was special, that she was beautiful, she was so willing to believe him."

"Who are you talking about?" I gripped his arm.

"I saw him kiss her at the resistance camp. When she was on her own, I asked her what was going on," he explained in a dreamy, far-off manner. "I couldn't believe my eyes. Why would she be kissing him? She swore me to secrecy and said that I wasn't to say anything."

"Who kissed her?" I demanded.

"So I didn't say anything," Isidor sighed, turning to look at me for the first time. "I kept my promise to her and now I wish I hadn't. You were right, Kiera, I saw them talking together beneath that willow tree."

I wanted to scream at him, *"Stop rambling – just tell me! Who was it you saw with Kayla?"* but I had waited this long for him to start talking, so I didn't want to interrupt him for fear that he might clam up again, so I let him continue.

"The night Kayla was murdered," Isidor continued. "They had been together. As I laid her in her grave, I could smell him on her. I don't know if he was the one who killed her, but they had definitely been together."

Almost on the verge of screaming at him, I took a deep breath and said, "Isidor, who is *he*?"

With a look of sadness, Isidor said, "I'm so sorry, Kiera, I wish I didn't have to be the one to tell you this as I know it's going to break your heart, but I think Elias Munn is -"

Before he could finish, there was a swishing sound like a blade being cut through the air. And then Isidor was clutching at his throat.

Chapter Twenty-Seven

Isidor's eyes spun in their sockets as he grappled at the wooden stake which was now protruding from his neck, just above his Adam's Apple. Blood pumped from between his fingers and ran from the corners of his mouth in thick, black lumps.

"Isidor!" I screamed as he wobbled before me.

Taking him in my arms, I cradled him against me. I looked around frantically to see if there was anything close at hand I could use to stem the flow of blood from his throat.

"Help me!" I screeched. *"Somebody help me!"* And it was then that I saw it: Isidor's crossbow propped against the wall in the gap we had slipped through earlier. Someone had shot Isidor with his own crossbow.

Isidor shook violently in my arms as if he were having a fit and his eyelids flickered. "Don't you dare die on me, Isidor!" I roared at him "Don't you dare! Do you hear me?"

Opening his eyes, he peered at me and made a gargling noise in the back of his throat. A black bubble of blood formed between his lips, then burst, showering me in a fine spray of blood. Knowing I was losing him and still desperate for answers, I lowered my face next to his and said, "Isidor, who did you see with Kayla? Who was it that betrayed her?"

His eyes flickered again, then closed. Shaking him by the shoulders and with tears rolling down my cheeks, I cried out loud, "Who did this to you?"

With his eyes still closed, Isidor took one blood-stained hand from his throat and gently ran it down the length of my face, taking my tears with it. Then, his hand flopped away and he fell still in my arms.

"No!" I screamed until my throat felt raw.

With my arms around him, I pulled him close, and all I could do was cry. I felt as if my heart had been crushed inside of me. "Isidor, wake up! Please," I begged him. "I can't lose you *and* Kayla! I can't!"

I looked down into his face and could see those black

flames tattooed up his neck now smeared crimson. His little tuft of beard jutted out and his eyebrow piercing gleamed green in the light of the roots that hung down from above us.

"Isidor," I sniffed. "Please don't leave me – *please!*"

But there was only silence apart from the drip-drip sound of the roots behind me. For how long I sat there and cradled him, I didn't know. It was probably only minutes or perhaps just seconds before the others came running.

Coanda was first through the gap and onto the ledge, Luke at his heels.

"What's gone on here?" Coanda asked, but I was too numb to say anything.

Luke rushed over and gently took Isidor from me. I was reluctant to let him go at first, but Luke prised him from me. I watched as he laid Isidor out upon the floor and pulled the stake from the puncture wound in his neck. He then laid his head against Isidor's chest as if checking for a heartbeat. Slowly, Luke raised his head and looked at me.

"What happened?" he asked, sounding breathless. "Who did this?"

"You tell me," I spat, and Luke recoiled as if my voice was full of venom. "One of you is a fucking killer and I want to know who!"

"Kiera, what are you talking about?" Luke asked, his eyes wide as he stared at me.

"Can't you see what's happening here?" I hissed, getting to my feet. "First Kayla, now Isidor - we're being picked off one by one! There's a freaking murderer amongst us and it isn't me!"

"Kiera," Coanda started, coming towards me. "What happened?"

"What do you think happened? Are you fucking blind?" I barked in sheer disbelief at him. "Somebody shot Isidor with his own crossbow!"

"But why would anyone want to do that?" he asked, glancing down at Isidor's corpse then back at me. "It doesn't make any sense."

"Isidor thought he knew who had murdered Kayla," I started, looking at both Luke and Coanda. "Apparently, whoever killed her had become close to her in the last few days of her life."

"But who was it?" Luke demanded.

"You tell me, Luke," I said staring into his eyes. "It could've been you who killed her."

"It could've been - but it wasn't..." he said flatly.

"And what about you, fly-boy?" I snarled turning on Coanda.

"What's that s'pose to mean?" he shouted.

"We don't know you - apart from the wild stories you tell about yourself, none us *really* know you. It was you who led us out here. It was your idea to come to the Light House. And why didn't you really want me to tell anyone? Huh? Was it so you could murder us one by one and no one would ever know? You could be Elias Munn!"

"And what about you?" Coanda said. "We only have your word that Kayla died the way you said she did. It was only you who examined her body. That could've all been some elaborate show just to hide your own tracks."

"Oh my god!" I gasped. "That's ridiculous'!"

"Is it?" Coanda went on and even Luke was now eyeing me with a look of distrust. Or was that just my own paranoia kicking in? "It's you standing there with Isidor's blood on your face and hands. The crossbow is just over there in that gap, within easy reach I'd say. We only have your word that he told you this stuff about Kayla. For all we know, he could have been accusing you of being the one who killed Kayla and you silenced him before he could tell anyone else."

I stood and stared back at Coanda and Luke and both stared back at me. "Do you really believe that's what happened?" I breathed. "Do you really believe I could kill Kayla and Isidor? I loved them like a brother and a sister. Do you really believe this, Luke?"

He was quiet for a moment as if contemplating his answer. Eventually he said, "I don't know what to think anymore, Kiera. Everything seems to have changed."

"But you can trust me," I said, searching his eyes.

"Like I trusted you with my best friend, Potter," he

reminded me. "I honestly didn't think you were capable of doing something like that to me."

"Luke, you make it sound as if we were engaged to be married or something," I gasped. "We were good friends, that was all."

"I thought we were more than friends," he said. "I thought we had something special. You didn't turn me down when we were together in that underground lake."

"Okay, so I fell in love with Potter, your best friend, but that doesn't make me a murderer," I insisted.

"But it's okay for you to point the finger of blame at us?" Coanda asked. "And as far as I can see, neither of us have done thing to raise anyone's suspicion; yet you are happy to point the finger of blame at one of us. I thought you could *see* things, Kiera Hudson. Why can't you *see* who this Elias Munn is?"

"I don't know," I said, trying to mask my own frustration.

"Maybe he has already blinded you?" Coanda said.

"How?"

"With his love," Luke said, and I detected a note of sadness in his voice.

"You're talking about Potter again, aren't you?" I asked.

"Well where is he?" Luke asked. "No one has seen him since Kayla's dead body showed up. Now Isidor is dead and there's still no sign of him."

"Have you seen him since he disappeared?" Coanda pushed.

"No," I whispered.

"Is that a lie?" Coanda came at me again, and I felt as if I was being interrogated.

"No," I said again without looking at either of them. But of course it was a lie. I had seen Potter and he had told me he was going into hiding and that he would follow us from a safe distance. But where was he now?

Coanda came towards me, and leaning in close he said, "If I were you, Kiera, I'd take a very long look at your lover, Potter before you go pointing the finger at me again." Then turning, he growled at Luke, "Help me lay this boy to rest."

I watched them silently carry Isidor from the cave. Taking

135

his crossbow, I cradled it against my chest and began to cry.

I leant against the wall and slid to the floor where I rolled onto my side and closed my eyes. Taking my iPod from my pocket, I switched it on and began to listen to *Wherever You Will Go* by Charlene Soraia. I couldn't help but think of Potter and that cigarette end I had found by the weeping willow. Had he put it there? He knew me well enough by now to know how I worked – how I could *see* things. Had my love for him blinded me just like Coanda thought? I hated thinking like this about Potter but so many roads Elias Munn had laid led to him. Would he have murdered Kayla? But then I remembered how he had suddenly been so protective of her when I'd explained Coanda's plan to him. Why? The message my father had left for me in that book: *'One may smile, and smile, and be a villain!'* Half-smiling to myself through my tears, I wondered if that single passage didn't actually take Potter off the suspect list. After all, he didn't smile that often as he always seemed so cranky and pissed off.

With so many thoughts going around my head, it took me a while to fall to sleep but when I did, I said...

Chapter Twenty-Eight

"Sloat," and pointed a finger at the floor. The assistant helped me to dress and when he was done, he scampered to the other side of the mortuary. I looked over at the police officer and could see he had worked his radio free.

"SNOW!" I yelled through the hole in my cheek, which flexed in and out like a valve.

"Snow?" the officer asked confused.

"She's saying no!" the pathologist said. "She doesn't want you to use your radio."

"Too bad!" the officer said, raising the radio to his mouth. "I'm calling in!"

Something told me that more cops would be a very bad idea, so I stumbled towards him, falling against the mortuary table. The officer pressed the transmit button with a fat thumb. Seeing this, I placed my two fingered hand against the table and shoved it towards the police officer. In a blink of an eye, the heavy metal table was spinning across the mortuary, its legs screaming against the stone floor like fingernails being raked across glass. The table smashed into the officer's legs and pinned him against the wall. It hit him with such force, that the sound of his thigh bones snapping would haunt anyone who heard it for years. The police officer screamed and dropped forward, his forehead smacking into the mortuary table with a dull thud. The radio shot from between his fingers and spun across the room. Whirling round, I spotted it with my bloodshot eye. I staggered across the lab and buried the heel of my boot into the plastic panel across the front of it. The radio split open like an old wound, spilling its wires and microchips across the floor.

"Crwoss!" I said to the pathologist who cowered in the corner of the lab. "Crwoss" I said again, holding out my deformed-looking hand.

Knowing exactly what I wanted, the lab assistant grabbed the silver crucifix from an evidence bag and laid it on the mortuary slab. I picked Murphy's crucifix up with my two fingers and tried to place it around my neck. Fumbling with only five

137

fingers between two hands, I looked at the pathologist. Without saying anything, she came forward on her knees. She stood and fixed the necklace into place for me. The pathologist stared at my face. I could feel hair now sprouting from the bald patches that covered my head. It was black with threads of blue running through it. But it wasn't just my hair that was growing back. Stumps were now appearing where I was missing fingers. I held my right hand up and watched as the skin on my hands almost seemed to split apart as my fingers grew back. My right cheek felt as it were being pinched and pulled to the right as my mouth began to take shape. I could feel my teeth pushing through my gums and blood washed into my mouth.

I looked at the pathologist with my bloodshot eye and she looked away in revulsion. The cop had been right – I was reforming – almost as if I were being reborn in some way. The pathologist took one quick glance back at me, then turned and scurried back into the corner of the mortuary. I tightened my overalls about my waist, rummaging through its pockets. I found an iPod and a red bandana that was soaked with blood. Struggling, I placed the iPod back into my pocket.

The police officer was now lying on the floor, clutching his thighs and screaming in pain. His face was red and sweaty, and his eyes bulged in their sockets. The lab assistant still cowered in the corner of the room and couldn't take his eyes off me. I turned to face the pathologist, who didn't look scared anymore, but curious.

"Sank-you," I said, and as my mouth started to reform, so my words sounded more like I intended.

"What are...who are you?" she asked.

I looked at her, my red eye now weeping blood onto my cheek, which I mopped away with the bandanna.

"What do you want?" she said.

Then, the mortuary door crashed open on its hinges and two figures came rushing in and...

Chapter Twenty-Nine

...shook me awake. I opened my eyes to see Luke staring down at me. His face glowed green from the light shed by the twisted roots that continued to make that drip-drip sound.

"It's time we got moving," he said, and any anger and resentment I'd heard earlier in his voice was now gone. "It's dark out and Coanda doesn't want to waste any more time. He's eager to take out those Vampyrus that are guarding the Light House."

"He's crazy if he thinks the three of us can do it alone," I groaned, pulling myself to my feet.

"Are you okay?" Luke asked me.

"No, not really," I replied.

"I'm sorry about earlier, Kiera," Luke started. "If it helps, I don't really think you're a killer. You're the last person I would ever suspect of hurting Kayla or Isidor. I know how much they meant to you."

"It didn't sound like that earlier," I said, brushing red rock dust from my overalls.

"Well maybe we both said stuff we didn't really mean," he said. "But whatever has happened between us lately, we're going to have to put that to the side for the time being or we'll never get through what's coming next."

Luke then turned and headed back towards the gap in the rock. Before he was out of my reach, I took his arm and said, "Do you really believe that Potter is Elias Munn?"

Then, looking at me he said, "Like I said last night, Kiera, where Potter is concerned, I don't know what to believe anymore." Then he was gone, slipping between the rocks.

I took one last look back at those roots that hung from the ceiling of the cave like some intricate plant, and throwing Isidor's crossbow over my back, I slipped through the crack and back into the fracture beneath the ground.

Coanda was peering up into the sky which was now dark and shimmering with the glow from the stalagmites that hung down like ragged, prehistoric teeth. He heard me enter and looked in my direction.

"Ready?" he asked, and his voice was toneless.

"I guess," I replied, and looked over at Luke. "Where did you bury Isidor?"

"Down there," Luke said, pointing into the narrow passageway.

"I'd like to go and say goodbye," I said to him.

But before Luke could say anything, Coanda cut in. "There's no time. Anyway, all you can see is just a bunch of rocks. The ground was too hard for us to dig."

"I'm not going anywhere until I've said goodbye to Isidor," I said firmly.

"We don't have time," Coanda started.

Heading in the direction Luke had pointed, I looked back at Coanda and said, "No one's stopping you from leaving, I'll catch up."

Coanda grumbled something under his breath, but he was too far away for me to hear, and to be honest, I didn't really care what he had to say at this moment in time. I lowered my head and stepped into the passageway. Squinting, I peered into the darkness and just ahead, I could see a mound of rocks that had been piled on top of one another. The area in which they had buried him was cool, but all the while I could hear that drip-drip sound coming from the root in the adjacent chamber.

I knelt down beside the rocks which entombed Isidor. Words seemed inadequate, so I just sat in silence with my eyes closed. I didn't pray, I didn't know how to. Besides, what was left to pray for, when everyone I cared about was being snatched from me? But, one thing I did know was that death wasn't going to pass me by, either. In my heart, I knew I wasn't going to leave The Hollows alive. Perhaps somewhere inside of me, I had always known this was going to be a one-way trip. If I was going to die down here along with my friends, I wanted to die on my terms; I wasn't going to be cut down like Kayla and Isidor had been.

I took Isidor's crossbow from my back and laid it gently on top of the pile of rocks and whispered, "See you in a while crocodile." Then, getting to my feet, I went back to where

Coanda and Luke were waiting for me.

Chapter Thirty

"We're up here!" someone called down to me, the voice echoed around the giant crack in the ground we had sheltered in. I looked up and could see Luke peering down at me from high above.

Without any further hesitation, I placed one hand in front of the other and began to climb up the rock face. As I climbed, there was a part of me that just wanted to climb back down again, crawl back into the narrow passageway, lie down next to where Isidor was buried, close my eyes, and never wake up. It wasn't that I was scared of what was lying ahead for me; it was knowing that I had to make that decision. I'd already decided in my heart that I wasn't going to choose between the human race and the Vampyrus. And where did that leave me? If I wasn't going to choose between them, did that mean death? Well if it did, let me just die now then, and let the Vampyrus and humans fight it out amongst themselves. After all, I belonged to neither race – I was a half-breed just like Kayla and Isidor had been. I was the only one left. I didn't owe either race any favours – let them both be damned to hell for eternity- what did I care?

But that was the problem. That's why I kept putting one hand in front of the other so I could pull myself up that rock face. Deep down I did care what happened. I cared deeply about all those innocent people, just like the townsfolk from Wasp Water who would suffer because of Elias Munn. And that's why I couldn't really choose between the humans and Vampyrus, because I didn't want to be the one who caused suffering and pain to either race. Why me? Why had I been damned like this? If there was a God, I wanted to renounce him, I wanted to turn my back on him. I didn't want this. Why had He picked on me?

I reached the top of the fracture and holding out his hand, Luke pulled me up. Scrambling to my feet, I looked into the distance. The light from the Light House turned away from us and cast us into a shadow. The ash continued to float through the night and cover everything, including us, in its silver dust. A warm wind blew and my hair fanned out behind me. Covering my eyes with my hand, I peered up at the Light House and could see the same flock of Vampyrus circling like buzzards searching for food.

Pulling open his overalls, Coanda looked at us and said, "I count twenty, but there could be more. With the element of surprise on our side and if we act fast, we can take them." Then, flexing his back muscles, his wings unfolded from his back. Shaking his wrists, his claws sprang out, and when he glanced at me again, I could see that he now had fangs. "What are you both waiting for?" he barked at Luke and me.

Just like Coanda had done, Luke pulled the top half of his overalls apart, revealing his muscular chest and stomach. Arching his back as if in pain, Luke's wings sprang from his back and the tips trailed in the ash. Clicking his knuckles like a boxer preparing for a fight, his long, ivory-like claws shot from his fingertips. Luke could see me watching his transformation and it was as if he knew I was remembering those stolen moments we had shared together. Luke looked divine in every way. He half-smiled at me, and I saw his fangs glisten. I looked away, reached round, produced my claws and ripped the back of my overalls open. As if desperate to be released, my wings thumped out of my back and fluttered open on either side of me. Those black, bony claws snatched at the ash that fell all around us. Running the tip of my tongue over my front teeth, I could feel that my fangs had also come through.

Luke stood watching me, my wings rustling in the wind, my hair flowing back off my face. His eyes glowed green. "You look beautiful," he whispered.

"Oh please," Coanda cut in. "You're gonna make me puke in a minute. Save the lovey-dovey stuff for later, pretty boy." Then, without another word, he was rocketing away through the sky.

I smiled back at Luke and those feelings of guilt gnawed at me again. "Watch your back," I said in warning, and then I too was racing towards the top of the Light House.

I drew level with Coanda, and as he looked at me, he

shouted, "Drop!"

Looking left, then right, I saw two of the Vampyrus zooming in at us from either side. Luke swooped over me as I shot downwards. Banking, I immediately climbed sharply again, the wind and ash rushing past me. The two Vampyrus that had been heading in our direction zoomed beneath me and smashed into each other. On impact, the Vampyrus' wings became entangled and they spun out of control towards the ground way below. They screeched frantically as they fought to untangle themselves, all the while plummeting to their deaths.

Luke spun around in the air and roared, "Coanda, there are too many of them. This is crazy!"

No sooner were the words out of his mouth, when Coanda grabbed both of us and we were corkscrewing through the air in a desperate attempt to avoid another onslaught. I screwed my eyes tightly shut and gripped hold of Luke.

As we spun through the air, I heard Luke shout, "We're gonna die!"

"Stop whining and fight or I'll kill you myself!" Coanda roared at Luke. Sensing that we were both out of immediate danger, Coanda let go of us and said, "Now fight!"

I sped away, through the air in pursuit of a Vampyrus that had just raced past me. I looked back and could see Luke sweeping away after another Vampyrus. Looking front again, I screamed, as a black shadow raced towards me. Before I had a chance to react, it had hold of me. The shadow stopped fluttering and I could see who it was.

Potter winked one of his black eyes at me, and said, "Sweet-cheeks, two o'clock!"

"What's happening at two o'clock?" I breathed, shocked at seeing him.

"I'm holding a tea party," he smirked. "What do you think I mean when I say 'two o'clock'?"

I spun around in mid-air to face two o'clock. Without realising it, my claws were pointed out before me and I swiped them at one of the approaching Vampyrus. The sound of its bony ribcage snapping against my long, pointed fingernails made me wince as it flew backwards, spinning towards the molten lava. I watched as it plummeted through the sky and thumped into another of its kind which soared below. This Vampyrus fell backwards, pin-wheeling through the sky, the claws at the tip of each wing frantically clutching at the air as if in some way they could hold onto nothing and save itself.

My attention was drawn away from the freefalling Vampyrus as one of Potter's claws went soaring past my face.

"Whoa!" I yelled, spinning around to see Potter tearing away in a spray of black shadows. As he snaked back and forth through the air, he screamed in rage, and as he did, I prayed he wasn't Elias Munn. As if being able to hear my thoughts, Potter snatched a quick look back over his shoulder at me with his dead, black eyes. He grinned, then sliced off the head of an approaching Vampyrus. A jet of blood shot up into the air, then showered down again, covering Potter's naked chest.

Still, another and another came at him. I watched as Potter's claws ripped into the Vampyrus. They shrieked in agony and spun away. One of them almost seemed to roll onto its back as it clawed at the wound that Potter had opened in its swollen-looking belly. Its wings fluttered uselessly on either side as it spiralled through the air towards the ground. Another of the Vampyrus zoomed in close, banked sharply as if needing to gain momentum, then came racing back towards us.

"We're too outnumbered!' I shouted at Potter. Then, scanning the sky, I added, "Where's Luke and Coanda?"

Potter ignored me as he concentrated on killing the Vampyrus that sped towards us in unrelenting waves. I straightened myself and began to beat my wings, sweeping this way and that and clawing at anything that came near. I glanced at Potter and he looked wild – insane – and again I caught a fleeting glimpse of his dead, black eyes. They looked like they had when he'd killed Eloisa – soulless. He moved with such speed that he became almost a blur. Potter extended his arms on either side of his body and spun his claws like a set of helicopter rotary blades. He leapt through the sky, and as he went, he slashed at the air in several quick and precise movements, slicing through an approaching Vampyrus and removing its bony legs. The Vampyrus spat and hissed in anger as its legs floated harmlessly away. The loss of its legs caused the Vampyrus to fall into an uncontrollable spin, as if by losing them it had lost its ability to balance.

I searched the sky frantically for Luke and Coanda again, but couldn't see them anywhere.

"We've lost Luke and Coanda!" I warned Potter as I raced towards him.

"No we haven't, they're over there!" Potter shouted back, pointing ahead of us with one hooked claw.

I looked in the direction he was pointing and could see Luke straddling one of the Vampyrus as his claws sliced and whooshed through the air. Coanda was zooming back and forth, lunging at passing Vampyrus and ripping lumps of black flesh from them with his fangs. As each of the Vampyrus screeched in agony, Coanda roared insanely with anger and punched the air with his claws. He looked as if he was enjoying every second.

Luke swooped through the air on top of the Vampyrus as he cut and thrust his way through any of the creatures that dared to fly too near to him. Luke's arms moved with lightning speed. At no time, as he hacked and jabbed, did I see the slightest glimmer of emotion on his face.

My attention was drawn by the sound of screeching from above and I glanced up to see one of the Vampyrus racing above me. It was so close that I could see the long, black hairs that hung from its legs snagging in the wind. Before I had the chance to lash out with my claws, it snatched hold of Potter and was now racing away with him up into the air. Potter kicked out wildly with his legs, but he couldn't work himself free from the creature's grasp.

"Bring him back!" I hollered, as the Vampyrus soared away.

"We've got to get him back," I heard Luke shout.
I looked to my left and could see that he had drawn level with me and was hovering only a few feet away. Then he was gone again, driving on ahead and dissecting anything that got too close to him.

"I thought you hated him!" I yelled.

Looking back at me, Luke half-grinned and shouted, "I

don't want them to kill him, I want to do it!"

I could see Potter way ahead in the distance as he dangled beneath the Vampyrus, his arms and legs waving and kicking desperately about. Tucking my arms in beside me, the little black fingers at the tip of each wing clutching at the air, I shot after him. I banked to the left a little then to the right to avoid approaching Vampyrus. Then, with my wings beating so fast on either side of me that they were just a haze, I zoomed after Potter.

Giant Vampyrus dived towards me on either side. As I grew more confident in flying, I tried to do a back flip out of their way – but I still had a lot to learn. The aerial-acrobatic move I performed was more like a cartwheel, and I came crashing down on the approaching Vampyrus. With my claws extended before me to break my fall, I unintentionally skewered one of the Vampyrus in its fury belly. There was a popping sound, and I looked down in disgust to see the creature's entrails spill from it. They flew out behind the Vampyrus in a black stream, like an aircraft ditching its fuel. It screamed in pain and dropped through the air like a stone.

I glanced up to see Potter was only feet away from me now. I swooped along beside the Vampyrus that had hold of him and began to slash at it with my claws. The Vampyrus turned to look at me, its face contorted in a mask of rage. Its jaws flapped in the rushing wind and its eyes grew fat and wide.

"You can't win, Kiera Hudson!" the creature screamed at me, and hearing it say my name made me falter.

"Elias Munn has led you into a trap!" it roared.

"Where is he?" I screamed back over the roar of the wind that whipped all around us, and I clawed at the creature again.

Then, shaking Potter so savagely with its talon-like claws, the Vampyrus sent Potter flying through the air. I watched him spin away, and instead of unfolding his wings and soaring up, he continued to fall towards the lava below. He looked to be unconscious. The Vampyrus who had flung Potter through the air started to change shape. I watched in horror as its body rippled, its coarse, black hair fell away to reveal Phillips.

Chapter Thirty-One

"Oh Kiera, don't look so surprised," he mocked. "We knew you were coming. Do you really think we would protect the Light House with just a handful of us? The Light House is the heart of The Hollows."

"Who is he?" I screeched and flew at him, my claws tearing at his eyes. Smiling he flicked me away. I somersaulted through the air and came at him again.

"Look all around you, Kiera," he smiled. "You're trapped. You can't possibly win.

I looked around to see a mass of black clouds racing through the sky towards us.

Clouds? I wondered. *Do they have clouds in The Hollows?* Looking up again, I saw that they were changing, breaking apart, becoming smaller. But as my heart began to race in my chest, I could see that these weren't harmless pieces of vapour. Each tiny piece had formed into the shape of a winged creature, a Vampyrus. Then, as if being punched in the face, the nightmare I'd had back in the Ragged Cove where I'd been fleeing along the shore hit me. In that nightmare, or as I now realised it to have been a vision, the clouds had broken up into pieces, thousands of pieces, each one taking on the form of a Vampyrus, just like they were now. Everything that I'd seen in my nightmares – *visions* – was now finally coming true. And in that instant, I could see running feet – they were booted. I was in a car and there were sirens wailing all around me. There were scratch marks, screaming – oh my god there was so much screaming. I was being swept up into the air. I was falling, I was being chased and the visions faded.

I looked down at the hard-packed ground and in the distance I could see shadows racing across the wasteland that we had crossed. But just like the approaching clouds, these weren't really shadows. And as they raced forward, I could see their white faces, their red, burning eyes that gleamed like brake lights in a traffic jam. They were stripped to the waist and their chests looked bony and bent out of shape. A series of sharp, pointed ribs protruded through their pale, yellowy-white skin. These creatures were so sickly-looking, I thought they were ill in some way.

With my heart racing into my throat, I realised they looked strangely familiar. They looked like deformed copies of Kayla, Isidor, and me. They were the half-breeds Elias Munn had manufactured. Somehow, he had managed to produce them; not perfect copies, but grotesque imitations of us, like the reflections you see in those distorted mirrors at the fairground. That's why the facility had been deserted and only a few left behind. He had known we were coming and had moved them. The disc! How had I been so blind? On the disc there had been drawings, diagrams of glass-like coffins – pods – there had to be another facility where these half-breeds had been kept. Like Hunt had been used as a decoy, Munn had led us to Ravenwood and the deserted facility so his army could be hidden and a cure for the virus could be found. But whatever he had used, the cure hadn't been perfect.

The half-breeds' skin looked oily, almost greasy, and I imagined that it would be slippery to touch. Their heads were long and narrow, with eyes fixed into the sides of their faces like birds. Their mouths were stretched open as if they were permanently screaming and they were crammed full of black, razor-sharp teeth. From the tops of their heads sprouted large, black, silky feathers, which they wore like Indian headdresses, and I wondered if this hadn't been a side effect of the half-human and half-Vampyrus DNA not being decoded properly. Munn had created a tortured-looking race – mutants – that bore some tragic resemblance to Kayla, Isidor, and me.

"What have you done, you sick fucker!" I screamed and grabbed hold of Phillips.

"I think they look quite beautiful," Phillips smiled, looking pleased with himself as he started to wrestle with me.

"What did you use?" I screeched at him. "The DNA that Hunt used was corrupted with a virus. What did you use?"

"Don't you think we knew Hunt had deceived us? In your desperate attempt to leave the zoo, you cut your hands, remember?" he beamed. "You left some of that blood behind. We only needed a few drops, Kiera."

"But they're mutants! Freaks!" I roared at him in horror as we grappled with one another. "They're nothing like me!"

"And that's just how we want them," Phillips leered. "Jesus, I couldn't think of anything worse than an army of do-gooders like you, Kiera Hudson. We don't want our army to be weak like you! What happened to you, Kiera? You were meant to be the chosen one, a great leader, a warrior who was going to lead us above ground and destroy the humans. But instead we were sent some bleeding heart, someone who loves humans. You might have been raised by humans, but you are not one of them!"

"And I'm not a Vampyrus either, Phillips!" I spat, trying to claw at his face, but he was too strong and knocked my hand away. "I'm a half-breed!"

"And like your friends, Kayla and Isidor, you will die a half-breed," he barked. "You had it in your power, Kiera, to make your friends great, but instead you led them on this pointless journey. You could have made them true Vampyrus!"

"What, and end up like you?" I hissed, my face inches from his. "Bitter and twisted and full of hate? I'd rather they be dead, and so would I!"

Out of the corner of my eye, I saw Coanda sweep in beneath Phillips.

"Dead, you say?" Phillips laughed. "I can arrange that!" And then he was lunging for my face, his fangs spraying hot bile. With one deadly swipe of his claw, Coanda separated Phillips' his head from the rest of his body. Immediately, his head spun away, but it was as if for just a few fleeting seconds he was unaware of what had just happened to him. As his head flew away, Phillips' mouth was opening and closing as if he were trying to say something to me.

"It's a trap!" I roared at Coanda, pointing to the mass of Vampyrus that raced towards us through the sky, and the thousands of half-breeds that charged across the wasteland beneath us.

"I think you will find it is they who have been trapped,"

Coanda grinned back at me with a wild look in his eyes. Then, without wasting another moment, he reached into one of the many pockets of his combat trousers and pulled out a small, brass horn. Raising it to his lips, he tilted his head back and blew into it. To my surprise, no sound came out.

"Sonar," he winked back at me and blew on the horn again. Glancing down, I could just make out Potter as he clung weakly to a piece of rock jutting from the side of the Light House. As I watched, a Vampyrus swept in and knocked him from his perch.

"*Potter!*" I screamed, dropping like a stone through the air after him. I didn't know if I would be able to catch him before he crashed into the burning lake below. The approaching Vampyrus raced towards me from both sides. Lowering my head and tucking my arms in beside me, I leant forward and raced towards him in a complete nosedive. My descent was so rapid that I could feel my flesh rippling against my skull. But I was catching up with him, and the world around me, the red rocks and the Light House, became a blur as if I had left time and space. With only inches to go before I was racing alongside Potter, another one of those giant Vampyrus swept in and clutched at me.

Pushing myself forward, my bones were rattling beneath my skin so much that I thought they were all going to snap. I inched towards Potter, but the Vampyrus wouldn't give up and within moments, he was on me again. I reached out with my claws and thrust them between the Vampyrus' ragged-looking ribs. A jet of black liquid spurted from the wound and the creature let out an agonising moan. I withdrew my claws and the Vampyrus slowed, leaving me the opportunity to grab hold of Potter and yank him free of the lava that bubbled and seethed just feet below us.
I put one arm tightly around him. He seemed dazed and disorientated.

"Are you okay?" I shouted at him.

Potter looked at me and to my complete surprise, he lent forward and kissed me on the cheek.

"Thank you, sweet-cheeks," he smiled.

I looked at him numbly and with my free hand, I touched my cheek where he had kissed me.

"Why did you come back?" I whispered.

"I told you I was watching your back and you looked to be in trouble," he said.

"Isidor is dead," I told him." He was murdered.

"By who?"

"You tell me?" I asked him, not taking my eyes from his, looking for any reaction.

"Is this like one of those pop quizzes?" he asked. "Because if it is, Kiera, I don't know the answer. I didn't kill him. Why would I?"

"Because he was just about to tell me who Elias Munn was," I told him. "Apparently, Kayla got close to him just before she died."

"That's impossible," Potter snapped, pulling away from me, so he could fly solo. "I was looking out for her. She was with me most of the time."

"And that's what scares me," I told him.

But before Potter had a chance to say anything back, Coanda came racing towards us.

"Look, Kiera! Look!" Coanda was shouting.

I turned to see what appeared to be another giant wave of Vampyrus swoop down. But these were different, they weren't attacking us, they were attacking the other Vampyrus. And unlike the others, these Vampyrus hadn't taken on their natural form, they still looked human – well humans with wings – just like I did. They swept through the sky with the grace of eagles.

"Who are they?" I asked him.

"The resistance!" he laughed. "Damn! Have you ever seen such a beautiful sight!"

And they did look beautiful as they swept through the sky, their wings shimmering, muscles rippling as they attacked the Vampyrus. Within seconds, the sky above surrounding the Light House had become a battleground as Vampyrus fought with Vampyrus. Their fangs and claws sprayed blood as they tore and ripped at each other.

Then I saw him, Luke being chased by a flock of those black, bristling Vampyrus. They snatched and bit at him. He struggled with them, but he was outnumbered, and within moments he was spiralling out of the sky. A black shadow swooped in and snatched Luke away from the screaming half-breeds that waited below to tear him to pieces.

"What was that?" I asked breathlessly.

"Potter," Coanda said, as he hovered beside me.

I turned to where Potter had been floating just seconds before, but Coanda had been right, he had raced forward to save his friend. Again.

Chapter Thirty-Two

Coanda and I raced towards them as Potter carried Luke to a rocky hill away from the battle that was now raging. Some of the resistance had now leapt from the sky and were now battling with the mutant-looking half-breeds that rampaged across the wasteland surrounding the Light House.

As I soared over them, my heart raced like a trip hammer in my chest as I saw all those distorted imitations of my dead friends, Kayla and Isidor. They were hideous, and to look at them made me shudder.

They raced around at incredible speeds, leaping and throwing themselves at the members of the resistance. All of them had fangs in their misshapen mouths. Their eyes swivelled in pockets of blood. Their heads were kind of pointy in shape and some of them had gaping wounds that looked open and raw. I remembered the 'Isidor' half-breed I had seen in the facility and how it had something close to an umbilical cord protruding from the crown of its head. To see those mutants below me with those fleshy holes made me wonder if that's where their 'umbilical cords' had been ripped out.

Unlike Kayla, Isidor, and me, these mutant half-breeds didn't appear to have wings. Instead, their corrupted DNA had produced a cluster of black feathers that protruded from the backs of their heads, arms, and shoulders. They looked like a mass of crows that had been savagely plucked. Some of them obviously sensed that they should be able to fly as they launched themselves into the air at the resistance that rocketed above them. But their tatty-looking feathers were unable to keep them in the air, and they fell back to the ground in frustration. I even saw a few that didn't have hands at all, but three of those little black, bony fingers. All of them looked gaunt, ashen, and ill – like corpses that had been brought back to life.

Several had clumps of red flame-coloured hair, just like Kayla's, but it stuck from their heads in dry tufts. There were others that were a shattered reflection of me and they raced across the wasteland with streaky black hair flowing from them, but instead of it growing from the tops of their heads, it grew from their faces, necks and arms. They were all an abomination – creatures that had no place in The Hollows – no place in any world. I swept from the sky with Coanda and we landed next to Potter as he was getting Luke to stand on his feet.

Realising it was Potter who had rescued him, Luke pushed him aside. "Get out of my way, *friend!*"

"I just saved your bacon," Potter said.

"I was doing just fine," Luke snapped, unable to bring himself to look at Potter.

"Didn't look like that to me," Potter corrected him.

"Do me a favour, Potter, stop acting as if you are my friend," Luke snapped. "You're no friend of mine."

Potter glanced at me, and I said, "Luke knows about us."

"Oh," Potter said and looked at Luke.

"Yeah that's right, *friend!*" Luke almost seemed to snarl, showing his fangs. "I know all about you and Kiera."

"I'm sorry," Potter said going to Luke, and I could see that he looked concerned by Luke's obvious hurt.

Luke turned to face Potter and knocked his hand of friendship away. "How could you treat me like this?"

"I didn't plan this you know – it just kinda happened," Potter said.

"Exactly how did it happen?" Luke stared at him. "When did it happen?"

"Back at Hallowed Manor," Potter confessed. "In the Gate House."

"The Gate House?" Luke gasped. "I see – how very romantic. While I was healing up in the attic, you were making a play for my girl."

"Your girl?" Potter said, now sounding frustrated. "It wasn't like you and Kiera were engaged or anything."

"No, but you knew I liked her, though," Luke said, moving toe to toe with Potter.

Oh my God, they're going to start fighting in a moment, I thought and wedged myself between them.

"Just stop it!" I shouted at the both of them. "I'm not some possession, you know. This macho shit-head stuff isn't going to solve anything. If you two haven't noticed, we're in serious trouble here!"

"Well, just don't expect me to like it," Luke barked. "Don't expect me to like him!"

"The feeling's mutual," Potter quipped.

"Look around us – can't you see what's happening here?" I yelled. "We've lost friends, The Hollows is at war, and the Earth is soon to be invaded. You need to put your differences aside, for now at least, because we either stand and fight as one or we die alone."

"You need to listen to her," Coanda said, coming forward. "Take a look around you. My resistance is outnumbered; they will only be able to protect the Light House for so long. We need to get to the Dust Palace and fast. Only there will Kiera be able to tell the Elders her decision and end this."

Scowling, Luke and Potter stepped back from each other.

"Let's just get through this if we can," I said to them. "We can save our differences for another day – another time."

Potter took a cigarette from his pocket, lit it and drew in a deep lungful of smoke. "Whatever you say, sweet-cheeks."

Hearing Potter call me "sweet-cheeks", Luke shot a quick glance at him and snarled.

Potter shrugged back and said, "Well she has got the sweetest…"

"Stop it!" I shouted at him, knowing that he was just trying to bait Luke.

"Okay! Okay!" he half-smiled, holding his hands up as if in surrender. "I won't say another word."

"That will be a first," Luke cut in.

"And that goes for you too!" I yelled at Luke. "God almighty – it's like I'm hanging out with a couple of kids."

"He started it…" Potter said blowing smoke from the corner of his mouth.

"You started it back in the Gate House," Luke snapped back.

"I give-up!" I cried, throwing my hands up into the air.

"Coanda, just lead me to this Dust Palace so I can get this over and done with."

"Follow me," Coanda said, scrambling down the rocky ledge we had landed on.

I followed after him and looked up to see Potter and Luke climbing down behind me. They didn't even look at one another.

Once we had reached the cracked and ash-covered ground, we stood and watched the battle rage in the distance. The sky above the Light House was alive with Vampyrus as they fought one another. Even though I was some distance away, I could hear the sound of their giant wings beating and their agonising screams of pain and occasional triumph as they did battle with the Vampyrus.

On the ground, another battle was being raged as the mutant half-breeds ran wild, clawing at and feeding off the fallen Vampyrus. Coanda had been right, the resistance he had put together was outnumbered by the army Munn had grown, either be it artificially or by brainwashing.

I couldn't bear to watch those freaky imitations of Kayla, Isidor, and me anymore, so turning to face Coanda I said, "Which way is it to the Dust Palace and the Elders?"

"Over there," Coanda said, pointing in the opposite direction to the battle. "But I think we've got a problem."

"What sort of a problem?" I asked, turning to look in the direction that he was pointing. But I didn't need any answer from him to tell me of the imminent danger we faced as I looked at the wave of mutant half-breeds that were racing towards us across the wasteland.

Chapter Thirty-Three

They came at us, their eyes burning red on either side of their grotesque faces. They might not have been able to fly, but they had our speed. A wake of red dust and silver ash billowed up behind them as they raced towards us. Their claws gleamed in the orange glow cast by the lava that circled the Light House. The sky had turned a blood red and the stalagmites twinkled overhead like rubies.

We formed a line. There was nowhere else to go. We were surrounded from behind, in front, and above as a flock of Vampyrus swooped towards us. Potter spat away the cigarette that dangled from the corner of his mouth and flexed his claws as he readied himself to fight. Luke's wings beat behind him and he brandished his fangs.

"Do you have a plan?" I asked Coanda.

"No, but I do," someone said from above us.

We all looked up to see a tall, lone figure standing on top of the ledge we had just scrambled down from. Even with his baseball cap pulled down so that most of his face was cast in a shadow, it was his wild, yellow, gleaming eyes that gave him away. There Jack Seth stood. His emaciated figure silhouetted against the crimson sky.

"I thought you were dead?" Potter growled with annoyance at seeing Seth again.

"And you'll be glad I'm not," Seth said back.

"We don't need your help, Lycanthrope," Potter hissed.

"Are you so sure about that?" Seth smiled, nodding in the direction of the approaching half-breeds. "Your situation doesn't look good."

"I've been in worse," Potter grumbled.

"Time is running out," Seth reminded us. "Do you want my help or not?"

"Yes," I yelled, answering for all of us.

"Kiera!" Potter snapped.

"Shhh!" I told him. And however much it pained me to do so, I looked up and said, "Yes, we need your help, Jack Seth."

"On one condition," he smiled back, the red bandanna knotted about his scrawny throat flapping in the rising wind.

"Oh great, here come the conditions," Potter sighed.

"What do you want from us?" I called up to him, knowing the half-breeds were now on our heels.

"I come with you to the Dust Palace," he yelled back.

"No way," Luke cut in.

"Done!" I shouted. "Now get your scrawny arse down here and fight!"

Without wasting any further time, Seth stuck two fingers into his mouth and whistled like a man trying to attract the attention of his wayward dog. No sooner had he taken his bony fingers from his mouth, there came a rumbling sound which was so loud and violent, the ground beneath my feet began to shake. I looked up to see Seth tearing the flesh from his body in bloody strips and as he took on his werewolf form, a pack of giant wolves scrambled over the rocks and began to howl into the night. Their jaws were huge, like caves that were filled with razor-sharp teeth and thick, ropey lengths of drool sprayed from them.

Without needing any prompting from Seth, the werewolves leapt from the rocks and bounded towards the approaching half-breeds. The werewolves' bear-sized bodies shook with muscle and their fur gleamed crimson in the light from the Light House. With their colossal paws, they swiped at the half-breeds sending them flying through the air. Others lunged with their giant jaws, easily fitting the half-breeds' heads into their mouths. With a quick shake of their powerful necks they had torn the half-breeds' heads clean off.
Jack Seth leapt from the rocks and landed in front of me, and even though he stood on all fours, he was big enough that he could look squarely into my eyes.

"Thank you for coming to help us," I said, trying hard not to be caught by his stare.

"Don't flatter yourself, Kiera Hudson," he woofed at me, and the hair blew back off my face. "I didn't come back for you or your friends. I want an audience with the Elders as much as you do. I have my own race to think of and I want the curse that haunts us lifted." Then he was gone, bounding away, his giant jaws snapping and snarling at the first half-breed he came across.

"Doesn't that guy ever die?" Potter asked no one in particular as he stood and watched Seth and the other werewolves slice their way through the half-breeds.

"Perhaps he's hoping you die first," Coanda replied.

"Not today," Potter growled, springing into the air.

Without saying a word, Luke took to the air after Potter. Although they now had their differences, when it came to fighting the enemy, they stood shoulder to shoulder, their dislike for each other momentarily put aside. Coanda went after them, and I followed.

We were attacked from all sides, and it felt as if someone or something wanted to rip me apart, to devour me - kill me - from every angle. As a team we flew, ran, bit, and clawed our way through the mutant half-breeds and the Vampyrus that attacked from above. Soon, the hard-panned ground surrounding the Light House had become a bloody wasteland, littered with corpses. We pushed on, following Coanda as he cut through the battle. The air was filled with the deafening sounds of squawking, howling, and screaming. Werewolves leapt and bound, the Vampyrus beat their giant wings and the half-breeds fought with a frenetic energy that was close to madness.

Coanda cut a path through the half-breeds and we followed him into a rugged area of sandy-coloured stone. "We are never going to make it, there are too many," he roared over the sounds of battle. "Even with the help of the Lycanthrope, we are losing."

"Any suggestions?" Potter snapped, then he bit off the face of one of those half-breeds that looked like a deformed version of Kayla.

"We'll have to go via the Murka Tunnels," Coanda shouted.

"Have you lost your mind?" Luke roared as he gutted a half-breed with his claws.

"There is no other way!" Coanda said.

"What are these tunnels?" I yelled, staving off another

attack from the half-breeds.

"They are a labyrinth of passageways that stretch beneath The Hollows which are filled with a fog that is near impossible to see through."

"They don't sound so bad," Potter half-smiled.

"They are named the Murka Tunnels because of the murky fog," Coanda went on, ignoring Potter's remark. "But one wrong turn and you'll never find your way out."

"Sounds better and better," Potter said, driving his hooked claws into the throat of a passing half-breed. Blood jetted onto his face, and he wiped it away with his muscular forearm.

"But the fog is rumoured to drive you mad if you are in it for too long. Many have gone into the tunnels but never to be seen again, and they are believed to still be wondering around down there, driven to the brink of insanity."

"What a load of old bollocks," Potter grinned. "You've been reading too many James Herbert books."

"I've heard the rumours too," Luke cut in, shaking entrails from his claws."

Looking at Luke, Potter said, "Someone must have gotten out of those tunnels alive."

"How do you figure that?" Luke snapped, his anger with Potter still evident.

"How else do we know what these tunnels are like?" Potter grinned with that know-it-all smile.

Before they had the chance to start another argument, I got between them, and staring at Coanda, I shouted, "How do we get into these tunnels?"

"Follow me," he roared and was racing away across the wasteland as if there wasn't a moment to lose.

Chapter Thirty-Four

There were iron gates set into a nearby rock face. Over these, slats of wood had been fixed barring the entrance. Looking back over my shoulder, I could see that some of the frenzied half-breeds had broken away from the main battle and were now coming towards us. Seth stood on his back legs, rolled back his mighty head and howled at them. The noise that came from his throat was so deep that the ground shook and my bones seemed to rattle under my skin.

Potter and Luke stood beside him, dwarfed by his giant size. Baring their fangs and claws, their wings taut behind them, they slashed at the approaching half-breeds.

"Give me a hand with this," Coanda roared from beside me.

I looked and could see that he was trying to rip off the wooden planks that barred our entry to the tunnels. With the wind now blowing hard around us, I hooked my claws around the edges of the planks and pulled. They came away in splinters. Coanda gripped the railings of the iron gate and it shook in its frame.

"Pull!" he barked at me.

I curled my claws round the thick bars and with all my strength I yanked at them. There was some give and I could hear the rock beginning to crumble away around the edges of the gate.

"Hurry!" Luke shouted, his voice almost drowned out by the screaming wind and the cries of the half-breeds.

With my eyes shut tight, I sucked in a mouthful of air and pulled as hard as I could on the gate. Coanda pulled too, and at last I felt the gate come away from the rock face in a shower of red dust.

No sooner had the gate clattered onto the ground, Coanda was shouting at the others, "Into the tunnels! Into the tunnels!"

With more half-breeds coming at us, we dashed into the entrance of the tunnel.

"Bring down the opening!" Coanda ordered. "Seal the entrance!"

As if knowing exactly what he meant, Potter and Luke began to claw frantically at the walls of the tunnel. Then, I remembered how I had watched Potter close the opening to the tunnel that lay beneath the police station in The Ragged Cove. So following their example, I started to claw at the walls surrounding the entrance to the tunnels. Rock began to fall down and cover us in dust as the mouth to the tunnel began to fill. The half-breeds snatched at us with their claws through the hole, which was fast filling up.

"Faster!" Coanda shouted. "Fill the hole!"

Like desperate animals in their burrows, we raked at the walls with our claws, and I shot a sideways glance to see Seth pounding away at the rocks with his giant paws. It showered down in jagged lumps until we had closed the entrance to the tunnel and sealed ourselves inside. I could hear the half-breeds on the other side scrambling and scratching, desperate to find a way into the tunnel.

"We've got to keep moving!" Coanda barked from within the darkness.

I narrowed my eyes into slits and peered through the dark and could just make out his outline as he moved slowly into the tunnel. Then I heard the sound of fabric being torn. Within moments there was a flash of orange light as Potter flipped his Zippo lighter to life. He had ripped the sleeve from his overalls, wrapped this around a large splinter of wood that had come from the planks I had pulled down. I watched his face glow yellow as he held the flame to the torch he had made.

Smiling, he looked at me and said, "A smoker's way saves the day."

"That stuff will kill you," I reminded him.

"Yeah, and so will a lot of other things," he winked back at me.

Luke brushed quietly past us and began to follow Coanda down into the tunnel. Seth began to twitch and spasm beside us as he changed back into his human form. He looked at me, his yellow eyes glowing as fiercely as the torch that Potter held in his hand. Then, pulling the beak of his baseball cap down over his eyes, he walked away.

"C'mon, sweet-cheeks," Potter said to me and I followed him into the tunnel.

We hadn't walked far, when a dirty yellow fog began to swirl up from the ground and surround us. It had a bitter smell and choking quality. I covered my mouth and nose with my hands and coughed. But, the deeper we went into the tunnels, the thicker the fog became and even the light from Potter's torch failed to light the way. Something scuttled over my feet and I gasped.

"Take it easy, tiger," Potter whispered from within the fog," It was just a rat."

"I don't like rats," I told him. "And besides, it felt way too big to be a rat."

"God knows what's lurking down here," Luke suddenly said from beside me, the fog now so thick, I hadn't even been aware he had been there.

"That's just your imagination," Potter said back.

"Is it?" Seth grinned as he loomed up so close to me, that I could see the giant rat he held in his fist. It was the size of an overweight cat. The rat kicked wildly in his grip, its unnaturally long tail swishing back and forth. With his eyes spinning like two suns, Seth rammed the rat's head into his mouth and snapped his jaws closed. The sound of the rat's skull being crushed by Seth's teeth made me gag.

"You're so disgusting," I heaved and moved away, losing sight of him again in the yellow fog.

I continued forward, and as I did I was sure I could hear the sound of voices. It was faint at first, like children whispering behind their hands. Someone brushed past me, but I didn't know who.

"Potter?" I called out but he made no reply.

"Can anyone else hear those voices?" I asked, as the fog swirled all around me.

Silence.

Then, those little voices came again. It was definitely the sound of children – I was sure of it.

"Can anyone else hear those children?" I called out.

There was no answer, only the touch of someone as they

hurried past me, as if running.

"Who's there?" I shouted, now beginning to feel panicked and lost. Then, there was the sound of a scuffle, like two people fighting.

"What's going on?" I called out, my heart racing as I spun around on the spot trying to locate the sound.

There was a sudden cry as if whoever had made it was in pain. I turned towards the sound. There was more running as someone pushed past me, shoving me against the wall of the tunnel.

"Help me!" a voice sounded from somewhere in the fog. "Come quickly! He's dead!"

Chapter Thirty-Five

With my hands held out before me and my heart thumping, I staggered through the fog towards the sound of the voice that kept shouting over and over again, "He's dead! He's dead!" My ability to see through the dark had no effect down in Murka Tunnels. The fog was so thick and dirty I could just make out my own hand in front of my face.

I headed towards the voice as I cut my way through the murkiness. As I drew nearer, it lost its muffled quality and I realised it was Potter who was calling for help. I made my way as fast as I could towards him. And then through the smog, I could just make out the glow of his torch as he waved it back and forth through the air.

I reached him, and standing so close that we almost touched, he looked through the haze at me and said, "Coanda's been murdered."

"What?" I gasped.

"Take a look for yourself," Potter said, bending down.

I got down onto my knees, and put my hands to my face in shock. Spread-eagled against the wall of the tunnel was Coanda. He was slumped forward, his chin resting against his chest. Gently, I raised his head, and could see his dead eyes staring back at me through the yellow fog that swirled all around him. I looked down at the ragged hole in his chest and could see that his heart had been removed.

"Who did this?" I whispered, glancing over at Potter.

"I don't know," he said. "But take a look at this."

Holding up the torch, he passed it close to the wall just above Coanda's corpse. Written in blood above his head was this:

Kiera follow the sound of the children

"What do you think it means?" Potter asked me.

"Haven't you heard them?" I whispered.

"Heard who?"

"The children."

"What children?" he pushed.

"It doesn't matter," I said standing.

"What's going on here?" Potter asked me as he stood up, and as he did, I saw the hand that he held the torch with was smeared with blood.

"You tell me," I shuddered.

Potter glanced at his hand, and realising that I had seen the blood, he sighed and said, "When I found Coanda, I touched him. I thought he had stumbled and tripped in this goddamn fog – that was all. I must have got some of his blood on me."

Before I had a chance to say anything, Seth and Luke appeared from the smog. To be able to see each other clearly, we had to stand almost side by side. I felt Seth brush against me and I recoiled. He felt me flinch, and his eyes shone at me from within the gloom and I could just make out his rotting teeth as he smiled with pleasure at the thought of repulsing me.

"What was all the shouting about?" Luke wheezed as if choking on the fog.

Potter held the torch over Coanda's head. "Now we are three," he said.

"Four," Seth corrected him.

"I'd forgotten all about you," Potter said dryly.

"Who killed him?" Luke asked.

"I wonder?" I said, peering at Potter. With our number depleting by the hour, the list of suspects was growing smaller and smaller. I didn't have to *see* anything to know that the killer – this Elias Munn – was either Luke or Potter. But to even think that made my heart ache. How could either one of them be Elias Munn? It couldn't be possible – I would've seen it. But there was one other, and I glared at Jack Seth through the smog. I had believed him to be dead after Potter had pushed him over the cliff edge. But he had survived and had followed us. Maybe that's who Kayla had heard following us. But would Kayla have fallen for Seth? He was an ugly, disgusting child killer. Then, seeing his eyes spinning through the fog, I understood how he got Kayla to fall in love with him.

"I love you," she had said to whoever had been hiding behind the weeping willow. Seth had entranced her with his stare. Isidor had said how he couldn't understand how Kayla had grown close to this person. She hadn't fallen in love with him at all. Seth had tricked her like his son had tricked his victims – those women he had butchered. With my heart racing in my chest, I understood why Kayla had undressed just before being murdered. Seth had seduced her with his stare. He had made her want him, just like he had made me desire him when I had looked into his eyes in the caves beneath the Fountain of Souls. Even though I could see him torturing me, hurting me, I had still seen myself undress for him, lay down for him and let him take me.

"And what does that message mean?" Luke suddenly asked, but I hardly heard it. I couldn't take my eyes off the murdering Lycanthrope.

"Maybe you should ask him?" I said, pointing at Jack Seth.

"Me?" Seth sneered, with a bemused smile on his face.

"Or perhaps I should call you Elias Munn?" I whispered in shock.

"What are you going on about," he barked. "I know these tunnels are believed to be filled with a fog that can drive you insane, but I had no idea the effects would take hold so fast."

Ignoring Seth, Potter looked at me and said, "What are you talking about, Kiera?"

"Jack Seth is the killer -"

"We've known that for years," Luke cut in.

"No!" I snapped. "He's responsible for killing Kayla, Isidor, Coanda, Murphy and all the others that have lost their lives…"

"I didn't kill Murphy," Seth spat. "That was Phillips, you saw him…"

"No, but you led us to him," I cut over him. "It was you who told Murphy that we should pay a visit to that monastery where we all nearly lost our lives. How have I been so dumb? How have I not seen it?"

"I don't have to stand here and listen to…" Seth started, but before he'd had the chance to finish, Luke and Potter had taken hold of him. "This is an outrage," he struggled.

"That's the real reason you wanted to get to the Dust Palace because you haven't been able to get me to fall in love with you," I said. "So many times you've looked into my eyes and shown me the perverted pleasures you have to offer. You hoped that I would fall for you. But each time I've resisted, so now your last chance is to get inside the Dust Palace and kill the Elders."

Then, fixing me with his stare, he looked into my eyes and said, "You stupid girl, you didn't resist me. It was I who resisted you. You couldn't have stopped me from taking you if I'd really wanted you. Nothing could have stopped that. But you were my test, Kiera Hudson. To be able to resist you, to not take you, rip you apart, eat you every time I laid eyes on you, told me that I could be redeemed, that I could fight my desire to kill and butcher."

"I don't believe you could resist killing anyone," I hissed. "Potter was right, you are murdering scum and you deserve to die for what you've done."

"Then kill me," he suddenly growled, and struggled free of Luke's and Potter's hold. "If you really believe that I'm Elias Munn, kill me now." Ripping his bandanna from his throat, he threw it at me and bared his neck. "Go on, suck the life out of me, you bloodsucking vampire bat, because that's what you are!"

With images of Kayla and Isidor racing across my mind, I lunged at Seth and sunk my fangs into his ropey-looking neck. His hot blood washed over my tongue and down my throat, where it burnt like acid. Then, as Seth writhed against me as if gaining some morbid pleasure from me feeding off him, I heard those children's voices again. But this time they were closer, as if whispering in my ear.

"No, Kiera," their voices sung softly all around me. "Bring the Lycanthrope to us and you will *see* all." Then, those children, if that's really what they were, giggled and were gone again.

Opening my eyes, I took my mouth from Seth's neck.

"What did you hear?" he asked me as I stepped away, wiping his blood from my lips with his red bandanna and placing it in my pocket. Continuing to stare at me, he said, "You heard them, didn't you? You heard the children."

"What children?" I gasped, feeling out of breath.

"You heard the voices of the gods," he said.

"The gods?" I asked, feeling light-headed.

"I heard them once before," he said. "The day they cursed me and my race. And that's my reason for wanting to seek an audience with them; I want to beg them to lift the curse they placed on us all those years ago."

And then as if being haunted by ghosts, I heard the sound of those children's voices again, whispering and playfully giggling amongst the fog. I turned my back on Seth and peered into the yellow vapour that swirled all around me. The voices came again, but this time they were fainter as if moving away from me. I followed the sound through the tunnel.

"Hey, Kiera!" Potter called out from behind me. "What are we doing with the wolf man?"

"Bring him with you," I said. "But don't let him leave your side."

"Easier said than done in all this fog," I heard Luke say.

But I didn't stop, I just followed those voices.

Chapter Thirty-Six

Through the tunnels I went, not knowing where I was going or what direction I was heading. It didn't seem to matter to me. For some reason I trusted those innocent-sounding voices. I could hear Potter, Luke, and Seth behind me as they followed the sounds of my footsteps echoing back down through the tunnels. Could they hear the voices? I doubted it or they would have asked me about them. No, these children, whoever they were, were only talking to me – guiding me.

I don't know for how long I followed the voices through the labyrinth of tunnels, but eventually the fog started to thin out and eventually evaporate. There was a dim, orange light at the end of the tunnel, and I sped up.

"Where are you taking us?" Potter called out.

Ignoring him, I raced forward towards the light. Stumbling out of the tunnel, I gasped in a mouthful of air, glad to be free of the suffocating smog. Blinking in the light that now bathed me, I looked ahead. The others stumbled into the light and coughed and sputtered as they gasped in lungfuls of fresh air.

We stood in a narrow valley which ran between two vast cliffs that towered above us on either side. But unlike the red rock that seemed to make up so much of The Hollows, the cliffs were a dull grey as if they had had their colour sucked from them. The sky above us was a black void. There were no twinkling stalagmites here. The orange glow that illuminated the valley came from the ground, which was covered in a similar type of moss I had seen back at the resistance camp. Just like the ground there, this was spongy, like a luxuriant carpet. At the opposite end of the valley, I could see what appeared to be four giant pillars sculpted into the rocks. Set between these pillars was a rusty-looking door that stretched up for as far as the eye could see.

I looked at the others and said," The Dust Palace?"

"I guess," Luke shrugged.

"What are we waiting for?" Seth barked, keen to get going and have his curse lifted, if that was his true reason for wanting to get inside there.

"Watch him," I said to Luke and Potter, as I set off across the valley.

The others followed at a distance, Seth sandwiched between Luke and Potter. A cool breeze fused with sand meandered about us, and our wings rippled. The sound of the children laughing had faded. It was as if they had led me this far, but had now disappeared, leaving me alone to find my own way into the Dust Palace.

Before the giant door stood several stone steps. Placing my foot on the first, I looked back at the others as they joined me.

"Are you sure about this?" Potter asked, taking me to one side so that we were out of earshot of the others.

"I'm not sure of anything anymore," I whispered looking up into his dead, black eyes.

"Does that include me?" he asked.

Not knowing what lay ahead on the other side of the door and fearing this could be our last moments together, I said, "I do love you." Then, I headed up the steps.

As I climbed them, I could see that the building set into the rocks wasn't made of stone at all, but of smouldering ash. It glimmered red as if on fire, and wispy trails of smoke seeped from the cracks that covered it. I could hear a hissing sound as if the palace was on fire, or at least smouldering. Heat radiated from the building, but oddly I felt cold. I reached the giant door that towered high above me and could see it was coloured brown with scorch marks, as if at some time in the distant past it had been set on fire. The door was open, just enough for me to step through.

The others joined me on the top step and there was an eerie silence between us. Not one of us said anything, and we all shared a nervous glance. Even Potter seemed to have lost that cocky look of his, the arrogance melting away before the Dust Palace. None us had to speak, there were no words that could explain the seriousness of what was about to happen – the gravity of the decision I was going to make on the other side of the door we now stood before.

Every step I had taken since arriving at The Ragged Cove

had been leading me here, to the Dust Palace, the home of the Elders, where I would decide the fate of two races. Both good, both bad, both capable of true greatness, if only they had someone to show them the light.

I looked at Luke and his face was ashen, gaunt, and tired. Potter took a cigarette from his pocket, stuck it in the corner of his mouth, then spat it out as if thinking better of it. Seth stared at the crack in the door, his eyes burning bright.

There was only the four of us left; only the four of us had made it this far. Two Vampyrus, a Lycanthrope, and one half-breed. An unlikely quartet, one of which was a traitor. Who was it and how many of us would leave the Dust Palace alive?

Not knowing the answer to my own questions, I slipped between the gap in the door and entered the Dust Palace.

Chapter Thirty-Seven

A long, stone corridor lay before us. The walls were lined with a thousand or more candles. As the last of us stepped into the Palace, the door slammed shut behind us and a thousand flames flickered, casting shadows up the ashen walls. There was only silence and it was louder than any sound I had ever heard. The four of us stood side by side and looked straight ahead. My heart was racing so fast inside my chest that I thought it might just explode at any moment. Without saying a word, I took a deep breath and stepped forward.

The floor was made of burning coals and they hissed and spat with every step I took. But my shoes didn't smoulder or perish; in fact, like the rest of me, my feet felt cold, as if I had just plunged them into a tub full of icy water.

The four of us moved forward, not one of us daring to say a word. We came to the end of the corridor and found ourselves in a vast chamber that didn't look to dissimilar to the inside of an ancient cathedral. Ash-covered pillars stretched up into the ceiling which looked as if it had been constructed from hundreds of seething, wooden beams. It was as if the whole palace was slowly smouldering like the embers of a dying campfire. Just like the many cathedrals I had visited, this had an altar that was on a raised platform. It was supported on four raised legs, as if the altar itself was set inside some kind of smaller temple. Before it stood four robed figures and their faces were covered with hoods.

"Welcome to our home at last, Kiera Hudson," one of them said, and although they were the size of adults, the voice was that of a little girl, no older than six years.

With goose flesh running up my spine at the sound of the Elder's voice, I knew that it was the same as the voices I'd heard in the tunnels. I looked at the four of them and because their faces were shrouded, I couldn't tell which one of them had spoken.

"You have done well to have come so far," one of them said, but it was a different voice this time, the voice of a small boy.

"You have *seen* much, but you have been *blind* too."

"Blind?" I whispered.

"Oh, Kiera," another of them said from beneath their hood in a child's voice. "Can't you *see* what you have done?"

"I don't understand," I said.

"You've led our enemy – Elias Munn – into our home," one of them said.

I glanced along the line at Potter, Luke, and Seth, then, turning to face the Elders I said. "I've seen who this Elias Munn is," I told them. "You are right, he is amongst us and his name is..."

"Shhh," one of the Elders said, then giggled in a childish way. "Let's see if you have seen right, Kiera Hudson."

There was a pause of silence before one of the Elders said in a small voice, "Will Elias Munn please step forward."

I shot a glance down the line and none of them moved. I looked at all of their faces as they stared straight ahead at the Elders. None of them seemed to show any emotion, their faces passive, lifeless.

With my blood beginning to boil, I stood in front of Seth and hissed, "Go on, reveal yourself. I know it's you."

Jack Seth just stared back at me, his eyes gleaming yellow and crazy as ever.

"Tell them that it is you," I demanded, and tugged at his arm. If he wasn't going to step forward, then I would drag him before the Elders myself.

Then, from the corner of my eye, I saw someone move. With my heart aching in my chest, I watched Potter take a step forward.

Chapter Thirty-Eight

"No!" I gasped, turning to face Potter. "Tell me it isn't true."

Potter just looked at me with his dead, black eyes. His face was devoid of all emotion.

Taking hold of him, I shook him and screamed, "It's not you Potter! Tell me so! Talk to me!"

Then, without taking his eyes off mine, he opened his mouth as a thin, black line of blood ran over his lips, down his chin, and splattered onto his naked chest.

"What's going on?" I gasped in confusion. And it was as I looked at the blood running down his body that I saw the fingers sticking out of the hole in the centre of his chest. Clutched between those fingers, was something red and black, and it pulsed in and out.

Not understanding what I was seeing, I watched the hand disappear again.

"Potter?" I groaned as he slumped forward into my arms to reveal my mother standing behind him. She stood clutching Potter's heart in her fist.

"Oh, my god, what have you done?" I mumbled, still unable to comprehend what was happening.

"He was in the way," she smiled down at me as I lowered Potter to the ground.

"In the way of what?" I breathed, my mind still trying to make sense of what was happening.

"The person who really loves you," she said, dropping Potter's heart to the floor. "A good mother knows who is right for her daughter and it wasn't Potter. Elias Munn is who you are destined to love."

"What are you talking about?" I screamed at her, my mind now realising that she had killed Potter so I would be free to love Elias Munn.

"Elias loves you, Kiera, but you've just been too blind to see that," she said.

I looked down at Potter's face as he stared blankly back at me from my lap. *"But it's Potter that I love,"* I screeched. "What have you done? Oh my god, what have you done to him?" Not needing any answer from her, I pulled Potter up and cradled him against my chest. "No! No! No! Wake up, goddamn it!" I cried, tears falling from my eyes onto his upturned face. But Potter just flopped lifelessly back in my arms. *"You can't die!"* I screamed at him. "We were going on our first date when this was all over. You promised me! You were going to tell me what your favourite food was!" I shook him again, hoping I could make him come alive, but in my heart I knew he was gone. He had left me and I just wanted to curl up and die.

"He could never have made you happy," my mother said, as she looked down at me, her face pale, older-looking, and the ends of her raven black hair turning grey.

I looked at her and the sight of her disgusted me. With tears rolling down my cheeks, I sobbed, "Potter did make me happy. So happy you could never know."

"Nonsense," my mother snapped at me and I just wanted to rip her fucking throat out. "Your destiny lies with Elias."

"Who is he?" I roared at her.

"I'm Elias Munn," a voice said, and I turned to see Luke looking down at me. "I love you, Kiera, I always have."

I laid Potter's body on the ground, then springing to my feet, I lunged at Luke. *"You!"* I screamed. "It was you the whole time!"

"I love you, Kiera," he said again, grabbing hold of me. "We are meant to be together."

"Get off me!" I screamed at him. *"Get your fucking hands off me!"*

"Kiera, I know you love me too," he smiled. "You were so close to telling me in the underground lake. You know it in your heart to be true."

"I hate you!" I screamed into his face, spittle flying from my lips and showering him. *"I hate you! I want to rip your fucking heart out!"*

Then, gripping me like a bear, he leant forward and kissed me on the mouth. I tried to resist but my attempts to fight him off were fruitless. It was like he was sucking my strength from me. I kicked wildly against him at first, but my legs grew weaker and weaker until eventually I closed my eyes and just let him kiss me.

Just as if a thousand flash bulbs were popping inside my head, I saw myself in Kristy Hall's open grave. I called for Luke but he was gone. *Where was he?* I wondered. Shadows flickered above me as I climbed from her grave. Then as if watching from above, I saw myself being chased across St. Mary's graveyard by Kristy Hall. Then I was in the police car trying to escape as she smashed the windscreen with her face, desperate to get me.

But where was Luke? I wondered again.

Then, I could see him. There he was, watching from the doorway of St. Mary's church, but he was with someone else – Father Taylor.

"Let's see if Kiera is as resourceful as we've been led to believe," Taylor said to Luke. But Taylor had been deceived too, he didn't know who it was that hid in the shadows next to him, for Luke's face was masked in that shadow I had seen so many times in my nightmares.

Then, Kristy Hall was exploding in a shower of dust, as I watched myself thrust the crucifix into her tongue.

"She's good," Taylor smiled at the figure that loomed beside him. Then Luke was fluttering away in a spray of shadows and I could see him running to my rescue. I could see his black police boots in the rear view mirror as he approached the police car.

Another of those flash bulbs popped inside my mind. I could see myself staggering away from my little red Mini that had become stranded on the road that led from The Ragged Cove. I was running away from vampires in the snow as they were chasing me. There was a shadow in the sky and it was moving fast. It was killing the vampires, it was Luke and he was rescuing me. But he wasn't really rescuing me, he was stopping me from leaving The Ragged Cove; he was taking me back there so he could get me to fall in love with him. He needed me to love him so that the decision I had to make could be his.

The flash bulbs went pop again, and I was being dragged through the sky above St. Mary's Church by Phillips. We were diving towards the burning steeple and I saw Luke take his chance. He could save me, but that meant sacrificing one of his agents, but what did he really care, he had armies of them. So saving me and scolding himself, he made me think that he was selfless, that he truly loved me. And he sacrificed Rom too as he ripped him to shreds in front of the church – how would I ever expect that he was one of my enemies if he slaughtered one in front of my very eyes?

Then I was in Hallowed Manor, and I could see him through his window as he skulked in the darkness of the attic. He wasn't hiding because of the burns he had received saving me at St. Mary's Church, he was sneaking away at night, returning back to The Hollows to organise his agents as he knew the time was close. He had to pretend he was hiding away up there or his friends would have wondered why he kept disappearing. But all the while keeping me close, that's why I was really brought to the Manor – I could *see* that now.

"We must bring Kiera here," he had told Potter and Murphy. "She isn't safe without our protection."

So Potter and Murphy agreed to his plan and tricked me to going to Hallowed Manor on the pretext of watching over Kayla.

But why hide away at the Manor? Because that's where Doctor Hunt and Ravenwood were working on the cure for the half-breeds. He had positioned himself close at hand to steal it when their work was complete.

But Doctor Hunt suspected a traitor was close by so he had to be disposed of. Luke had him kidnapped, but left Ravenwood to work on the cure. But Taylor was a wild card and didn't follow the plans that Luke, as Elias Munn, had ordered. Taylor had started to bring vampires to the Manor and the situation became dangerous. So from his hiding place and unaware of his true identity, Luke manipulated Taylor and Phillips to invade the Manor, this would give Luke a smokescreen to slip away, meet with Sparky, kill the half-breeds and take Ravenwood back to the facility where Hunt was being forced to work on the cure. He gave Phillips instructions to take Kayla, as he needed a healthy half-breed to test on.

When the fight was over, I watched from above as Luke came back to the Manor, pretending that he had flown after Phillips in an attempt to rescue Kayla. He had deceived us all. But not Murphy.

The lights flashed inside my head again, and I was in the signal box next to the disused railway line. I was secretly awake and listening to Murphy tell Potter that he suspected a traitor amongst them. But I hadn't been the only one pretending to be asleep that night – Luke had been awake, too. Knowing Murphy suspected a traitor, he knew he had to have him killed. With time running out and still desperate to get me to fall in love with him, he tried again to seduce me in the lake beneath the caves.

"Tell me you love me," he said, as I now watched like a secret spectator from the shore of the lake. But, I'd started to fall in love with Potter by that time, and I couldn't tell Luke that I loved him.

Frustrated and fearing that Murphy might discover his true identity at any time, he engineered his disappearance when the vampires attacked at the Fountain of Souls. Luke couldn't risk being anywhere near when Murphy's life was taken, so, pretending he had died at the hands of vampires, he skulked away until his agent, Phillips had murdered Murphy. Fearing he might never be able to get me to truly fall in love with him, Luke decided that if he could dehumanise me, to get me to see humans as nothing more than food, or better still, get me addicted to their flesh, then I would surely choose the Vampyrus to survive over the human race when the time came for me to make my choice.

So, revealing his true self to my mother and only her, Luke seduced her into feeding me that flesh – knowing that if I had one mouthful I would become an addict. I watched from above as Luke promised her a position of power in his new kingdom, and as he did he fed her own addiction with thin slithers of human flesh.

"You like this, don't you?" I saw him smile at her as she grabbed the meat from his fingers.

"Yes," she groaned as she gorged on the flesh.

"You wouldn't ever want me to take this away from you," he teased her.

"Never," she moaned.

"And you only want what's best for Kiera, don't you?" he whispered in her ear, as he fed my mother more of the flesh.

"Yes," she whispered, sounding intoxicated.

"Then help me," he smiled. "Help me to get Kiera to forget her human self and become a Vampyrus like us. You must feed her the flesh."

"I will," she smiled, as he brushed his lips over hers, and the sight sickened me. How could my mother have been so weak? She had become nothing more than a junkie, prepared to sell her daughter to get her fix.

But she hadn't been the only one. With those flash bulbs still popping inside my head like paparazzi cameras, I saw Luke visiting Kayla in her cell at the zoo. Instructions had come to Phillips for her not to be given any of the red stuff, even though they had made her an addict. At night Luke would creep into her cell and supply her with some, pretending that he was putting his own life on the line by sneaking from his cell to help her.

"I risk everything to come here each night," he told her. And Kayla was grateful for his help. I could hear him warn Kayla not to tell anyone – not even me.

"Why not Kiera?" Kayla had asked him around a mouthful of flesh.

"Kiera wouldn't understand," he said. "Kiera is special – she is unique. She can fight her cravings and she will expect you to do the same. I don't blame Kiera as she is strong and beautiful, but we are not like her. We are weaker, we crave the flesh, but she will be able to fight it. So please, Kayla, don't tell her I've given this to you or I won't be able to get you anymore."

"I promise," Kayla said, nibbling the flesh that dangled from between his fingertips.

Then I was on the road again that led to Wasp Water, and I could see that Isidor and I had both lost weight during our time at the zoo, but Kayla hadn't and I now understood why – I understood why she hadn't been able to beat her cravings. But Luke had whispered something else to her on his visits to her cell. He had told her that she was beautiful and how those words felt like sweet music to her ears. For so many years she had been bullied at school, called 'stickleback,' so when someone as handsome as Luke told her how beautiful he thought she was, Kayla couldn't help but lap those words up as quickly as she lapped up the red stuff he brought her each night. He truly was her saviour.

Then, one night Kayla said, "I love you, Luke."

"You love me?" he smiled back at her, taking her hands in his. "Why?"

"You have been so kind to me," she said, looking into his eyes.

"And I love you too, Kayla, but like a sister," he told her.

"A sister?" she asked, sounding disappointed. "Don't you love me more than that?"

"Perhaps," he half-smiled. "But I can't think about that now. If we ever manage to escape from here, then perhaps my feelings will become clearer."

"What about Kiera?" I heard her ask. "Don't you love her?"

"I think she loves me," Luke told her. "So you must never tell her about this conversation. I will tell her when the time is right. You wouldn't want to hurt her, would you?"

"No," Kayla whispered, shaking her head. "I could never hurt Kiera, she's my friend."

"Good," Luke smiled, leaning forward and kissing her gently on the mouth. And then he was gone.

Then, I was in The Hollows, in the cave with Coanda. Kayla was waiting alone by a nearby cave. I saw his hands sneak from the darkness and pull her inside. She shuddered in his grasp.

"Kayla, I need your help," he told her. "I think Kiera is in great danger."

"How?" Kayla asked him.

"I need you to listen to what Coanda is saying to her," Luke said.

"But that would be wrong, wouldn't it?" she whispered. "You, know, to eavesdrop on somebody else's private conversation."

Taking her gently by the shoulders, I watched him lean in close to her, and say, "We don't really know this Coanda. He might be leading us into a trap. He might want to hurt Kiera." Kayla looked up into his eyes and he could sense her unease about carrying out his request, so pulling her closer still, he kissed her. And this time it wasn't a brotherly kiss, but that of a lover. He pulled away from her, and looking into her eyes, he said, "Please, Kayla, for me."

So, turning her head towards the cave I was in with Coanda, she relayed every word of our conversation to Luke. But, someone saw Luke kiss Kayla and the sight of it disturbed him. Unseen by Luke or Kayla, Isidor had been watching them from nearby. I watched Isidor, wide-eyed and opened-mouthed as he saw Luke kiss his sister. Isidor slunk back into the shadows and I could feel his heart beating, like a child who had stumbled across a secret they wished they hadn't seen. But not only could I feel his heart, I could see into it as he remembered stumbling across Luke and me naked together in the lake beneath the caves. I remembered the way his cheeks had flushed scarlet at finding us there. And that's what caused his heart so much pain as he stood, hidden by shadows, watching Luke and his sister kiss, how would he ever tell me – wasn't I in love with Luke?

Then, I heard Isidor's voice whisper against my cheek as if he was standing beside me, but he wasn't standing beside me, he was dying in my arms, blood streaming from his throat in thick, black streams, as Luke laid the crossbow between the gap in the rock then disappeared between it.

"I saw him kiss her at the resistance camp," Isidor had gargled in my arms. When she was on her own, I asked her what was going on."

I looked away; I couldn't bear to see Isidor die in my arms all over again, but then I saw him with Kayla, lying next to each other by the campfire halfway up the Weeping Peak.

"Please, Isidor, you mustn't say anything," Kayla whispered to her brother over the snapping and hissing of the fire.

"But what about Kiera?" he asked her. "I thought she and

Luke were together?"

"She likes Potter," Kayla told him.

"Then you should tell her about you and Luke," Isidor insisted.

"No, not yet."

"Why not?"

"Luke said he will tell Kiera when this is all over," Kayla told Isidor.

I watched from afar as Isidor, rolled onto his side and said, "I don't like it, Kayla, not one little bit."

As I looked at him, all those flashbulbs flickered and flashed inside my head, and I understood why he had been so quiet on our journey across The Hollows. He wished he hadn't seen Luke and Kayla; he didn't want to be the one who would have to tell me about their betrayal – he didn't want to see me get hurt. And in his heart, he was angry with the both of them. Then, something brushed my face and it was the leaves of the weeping willows as I made my way through them. I could hear sobbing and I moved towards the sound. Kayla was by the tree, and as I peered through the leaves, I could see myself watching her from the other side of the clearing. But from my new hiding place, I could see who Kayla was talking to.

"I love you," she whispered, and Luke smiled at her, that smile that made his face look radiant.

"You have to keep us a secret until Kiera has made her choice," he said softly.

"I know what I have to do," Kayla murmured. "I know the decision that Kiera has to make. I know I have to be strong until the end."

"Good," he smiled again.

"Then can we be together?" Kayla asked him, tears on her cheeks.

"Come to me tonight, Kayla," Luke whispered. "When we camp, come to me and we can be together tonight." Then, hearing me coming through the willows, he slipped back in amongst the trees, dropping a cigarette end as he went.

"I love you," she said again and I watched her bury her face in her hands.

The bright lights flashed again, sending pinpricks of light dancing across the inside of my eyelids. The spots of lights formed shapes, images that I didn't want to see.

Kayla was there, I could see her standing in the dark. She was waiting for him. Her wait wasn't a long one, as Luke came to her out of the darkness. She ran to him, and he took her in his arms, kissing her face and neck.

"Do you really think I'm beautiful?" she whispered in his ear, and I could feel the insecurities in her heart. How could Luke love her? She was the stickleback, right? The girl who had been ridiculed and mocked by her peers because she was different. She didn't deserve to be loved by someone like Luke – this only happened in books, in movies.

"You are beautiful," he whispered back, pulling her close and unbuttoning her overalls. He pulled them down over her shoulders and she made a murmuring sound.

"Luke, maybe we should stop," she protested gently.

"But you are so beautiful, Kayla," he said, as her clothes fluttered to the ground.

I wanted to scream at her – to tell her to run and never stop. But I was a passive observer, myself held prisoner in Luke's embrace as I was forced to watch how he had betrayed us, how he had murdered Kayla.

And although she felt embarrassed and uncomfortable, she couldn't help but feel overjoyed that at last someone thought she was beautiful. So, looping her arms about his neck, she let him kiss her face, her chest and his kisses were so gentle.

Then, she was pushing him away and folding her arms over her breasts in embarrassment. "Someone is coming," she whispered, reaching for her clothes.

"No..." Luke started.

"I can hear them," she said. "It's the same person who followed us up the mountain."

"It's just your imagination," he said, pulling her close again, but keeping one eye on the woods behind her, as if he were expecting someone.

"Please, Luke, stop..." she gasped as she tried to push him away, I could tell by her racing heart that she knew that

185

something wasn't quite right.

But before she could break herself free of him, Luke sunk his fangs into her chest and bit her heart. Kayla shuddered in his arms, then, went rigid. My mother appeared from the woods, a rucksack over her back. And as Kayla twitched in Luke's arms, she came forward and placed a hand over Kayla's mouth to stifle any dying sounds she might make.

Between them, Luke and my mother laid Kayla upon the ground. Leaning over her, as if kissing her one last time, Luke removed Kayla's ears with one quick swipe of his claws.

"Wasn't eating her heart enough?" my mother asked. But she didn't sound revolted, just curious.

"I want to send that fool, Coanda a message," Luke said, placing one of Kayla's ears in each of her hands. "I want to tell him that I know he was taking her to the Light House to listen."

"What about these?" my mother whispered, pulling an identical set of clothes from the rucksack.

"Help me put them on her," Luke ordered, lifting Kayla's feet and removing her boots.

"Why?" mother asked him.

"The kid, Isidor will smell me on her," Luke said. "He can't know that we have been together. If I ever thought he had found out, I would have to kill him."

"Kill him anyway," my mother said.

"I just might," he told her, smiling.

And as they redressed Kayla, I knew why Potter had seen Isidor sniffing his sister's body as he laid her to rest. But Isidor's sense of smell had been stronger than Luke had known, because even though Luke had gone to great lengths to hide his tracks, he had left a trace of his scent behind. In her hair, perhaps? On her flesh? I couldn't be sure but Isidor had smelt Luke. And as those dreadful images of Kayla flashed before me, I heard Isidor whisper in my ear again, "As I laid her in her grave, I could smell him on her. I don't know if he was the one who killed her, but they had definitely been together."

Isidor's voice faded into that of a child's – a giggling child. I looked around and I was in the Murka Tunnels again, and I could see through the fog this time. It was as if it wasn't there. I saw Luke run past me and as he did, he sent me flying against the wall. He didn't look back. He was so intent on finding Coanda – the last person who stood in his way. The person who had raised a resistance against him, the resistance that was now circling the Light House and battling his army.

Seeking out Coanda in the murky gloom, Luke wasted no time in removing Coanda's heart. Then, once dead, Luke dipped his forefinger into the hole in Coanda's chest and inscribed the message above the wall. Luke knew I could hear the Elders, but fearing I might believe them to be the ghosts of the insane that were rumoured to be blindly wandering the tunnels, he had to make sure I followed them as they would lead me – *him* – to the Dust Palace.

Chapter Thirty-Nine

With those flashes of light fading like lightning during a summer storm, I pulled my lips from Luke – Elias Munn – and stared into his eyes.

"I saw it all," I whispered. "I saw everything. But how come I didn't see it before – how come I didn't *see* you?"

Still holding me close, Elias Munn, for that was his real name, smiled at me and said, "The problem with you, Kiera, was you were only ever interested in what you could see at your feet. You were always looking for the smallest of clues on the ground, but you never looked up, you never saw the big picture. That was your mistake."

Looking into his eyes, I said, "And your mistake was Potter. You never saw him – me and him together. He stopped me from falling in love with you. Just like my mother said, Potter got in the way."

"But now he is dead," Elias smiled, "and we are alive."

"I'd rather be dead," I told him.

"Kiera, you are meant to see things," he said. "You're meant to be a visionary, so why can't you *see* what it is that I have to offer you?"

Squirming from his hold, I looked at him and said, "I can see, alright. I know what it is that you have to offer me. A lifetime of war, bloodshed, and heartache."

"There you go again," he half-smiled at me as if I were a child who just didn't understand. "I could give you the world, Kiera. You have it in your power to destroy the human race and let the Vampyrus live above ground – to create a kingdom. You can decide right now, Kiera."

"And what sort of kingdom will you rule over?" I spat. "A kingdom where you murder and kill those who don't believe in your twisted view of freedom? That isn't a kingdom, that's a dictatorship and I can't be a part of that."

"And if you chose the human race over the Vampyrus, then you become what you most despise – a killer!" he barked at me. "If you let the humans live, they will only continue to fight amongst themselves, destroy the planet and in turn, us!"

"You are no different from them. Look what you have done!" I yelled at him. "You've started a war. You've turned your own kind against each other. You're destroying the world that *you* live in. Your army is raging war over the Light House, the very thing that brings light to your world. Humans and Vampyrus are not so different. They just need to learn to accept each other."

"There you go again," he roared, and I could see anger and hate for me in his eyes. "You just don't *see* it! If only you could find it in your heart to love me, Kiera, then I could take the decision away from you. It would become my burden. It would be me who would have to carry the guilt of killing the entire human race." Then reaching out and stroking my face, he added, "Let me show you how much I love you, Kiera, let me make that decision for you. I can feel your anguish and unhappiness at the thought of making your choice. I can take that from you – relieve your pain."

I slapped his hand away, and hissed, "The only pain I feel is the heartache for the deaths of my friends Murphy, Kayla, Isidor and the man I was in love with, Potter. You wouldn't feel any pain at the thought of destroying the humans – you hate them because one of them rejected you. That's what this whole thing is about. It's about your pain – the pain you felt when your lover turned away from you. And the saddest thing of all is that you are hurting more than anyone because you have never known what it is like to truly be in love."

"But I loved her!" Elias roared, remembering how he had been rejected.

"If you had loved her, you would've set her free to find true happiness with someone else. But instead, you ripped out her heart and ate it so she could never give it to another." Then, stepping close to him, I looked into his eyes, and added, "I *see* you, Elias Munn. I *see* into your heart and pity you, because you will never know happiness."

I had nothing more to say to him, and I knew in my heart the choice I was going to make. So, staring up at the Elders, I said, "I'm ready."

But before the Elders spoke again in their childlike way, Seth roared, "Kiera, behind you!"

Then, as if time had slowed down, I spun around to see Elias Munn lunging through the air at me. With my claws before me, I punched my fist into Elias Munn's chest and curled my fingers around his heart. With it pumping in my hand, his mouth dropped open and he looked down at the blood that was now pumping from him.

"Kiera," he gasped, raising his head to look into my eyes. Then, his body began to shake as it distorted before me. His face changed shape, and it was as if someone else was looking back at me as I gripped his heart. Elias Munn's hair turned blond, brown, and grey. He had blue eyes, then brown, hazel, green. His face changed shape, plump, thin, long. He suddenly had a beard, a moustache and then a goatee. And as he changed in front of me, I knew I was witnessing the many guises that he had taken over the hundreds of years he had lived. Then at last, he looked like Luke, just as he had when I saw him for the first time, dripping with rain in the front office of the police station in The Ragged Cove. That boyish look, with his glistening green eyes, chiselled jawline and jet black hair. But it had just been a mask.

"I love you, Kiera," he breathed, and just for the briefest of moments, I thought I saw him smile.

Remembering what I had seen, how he had murdered Kayla and Isidor, and knowing that Potter lay dead at my feet, I ripped Luke's heart from his chest and said, "I know."

I watched him drop to the floor, his chest soaked black with blood, and I knew that in a sad way, he had loved me. Dropping his heart, I turned back to face the Elders.

"How do you choose?" one of them asked, and it was the one who sounded like a six-year-old girl.

Before answering, my mother came forward and threw herself at my feet. "Please, Kiera, choose the Vampyrus, I don't want to die."

I tried to kick her away, I didn't want her near me, I couldn't bear to feel her touch. But she gripped hold of my leg and began to sob.

"Please, Kiera, don't let me die," she wailed. "You wouldn't let your mother die..."

Gently, I prised her fingers free of my leg, and holding her face in my hands, I whispered, "My mother is already dead."

Snivelling, she crawled away towards Jack Seth who stood nearby. And even by his own murderous standards, he must have been sickened by her, as he moved away. I looked at him, and he stared at me with those yellow eyes.

"You might want to get out of here," I told him.

Shrugging his scrawny shoulders, he flashed his broken teeth at me and said, "Doesn't bother me which way you choose, I ain't human and I'm definitely not a Vampyrus." Then chuckling to himself, he added, "I didn't ever think I'd see the day when I was grateful for being a werewolf! No, knock yourself out, you make your decision. I'm gonna hang around for a while, me and the Elders have some unfinished business."

I looked one last time at Potter as he lay dead at my feet, and with tears in my eyes, I smiled at him and whispered, "I love you, Potter." Then, raising my head, I stared at the hooded Elders and said, "I refuse to choose."

"Oh, Kiera," the boy said. "You must choose – it is the path that you were born to take."

"I won't do it," I said flatly. "I will not decide."

"But you must," one of them giggled, "Even though Elias Munn is dead, his armies will still invade above ground. Munn will soon be replaced by another."

"I'll help them to find peace," I said, refusing to budge.

"But, Kiera, that has been tried before," the girl said. "That is why you were chosen, a half and half of both species to finally choose which race would live and which would die. A half-breed would understand."

"Choose the Vampyrus," I heard my mother whimper from the corner.

Ignoring her, I continued. "I will not be responsible for destroying an entire race of people."

"But by refusing to make a choice, you are destroying two races," one of them giggled again. "The Vampyrus are already creeping from the sewers, flooding the subways, and the crater is complete. Thousands are poised to attack above ground in moments. You must choose now, Kiera. Now!"

Then, looking at them, I said, "I'd rather die!"

"You can't die," one of the Elders mused. "Who is going to kill you?"

Turning my back on them, I slowly crossed the chamber and headed towards Jack Seth. His eyes met mine, and I stared straight back into them. They spun the brightest of yellows as if on fire. I wrapped my arms around his neck, and breathing into his ear, I whispered, "I'm all yours, Jack Seth." Knowing he wouldn't be able to stop himself once I had offered myself to him, I stared one last time into his crazy eyes and said, "Kill me!"

I heard a howl of murderous passion, felt razor sharp teeth sink into me, and then everything went black.

Chapter Forty

There was nothing. No light or sound. There was only weightlessness. I wasn't in pain, I wasn't happy or sad. Nothing. Was this what death was really like? Wasn't there meant to be some kind of tunnel? A bright light even? Where were all my friends who had passed before me? Weren't they meant to be waiting to greet me? Great beaming smiles to welcome me home? But there was something – I was thinking, having conscious thoughts. So that was like being alive, right? Like being in a coma, but not being able to move or speak.

"Oh no, Kiera, you're not alive. You really are dead," a voice said from beside me and without even turning, I could see that it was one of those hooded Elders who had spoken to me. But its voice no longer sounded childlike and playful. Now it sounded deep and old.

"The Lycanthrope mauled you to death," another said, and this time the ancient voice came from above me. "If only you could see yourself, Kiera. He made a right mess of you."

"And my mother?" I asked them.

"The Lycanthrope's lust for blood was unforgiving once he had eaten you," another of the Elders said, this time from beneath me.

"Where am I?" I asked them.

"Nowhere," the fourth replied.

Then, seeing them for the first time, they removed their cloaks and revealed themselves. But their cloaks didn't come fully away; they flew behind them like wings. I could see the fabric had been stitched to their flesh. It wasn't the only stitches I could see. Their decrepit faces and bony bodies were a crisscross patchwork of scars. They were hideous, and the sweet, innocent voices they had spoken with were no more than a deception to hide the true horror that hid beneath their robes.

"Where's nowhere?" I asked, fearing the answer.

"Kiera, you chose to end your own life over that of the Humans and Vampyrus!" the female of the Elders said, her face a writhing mass of wrinkles. "You saved two entire races even

though you were not one of them. And that is your true greatness! You're not great because you can fly, race at incredible speeds and see what others cannot. What you have truly seen is the potential goodness in both the Humans and the Vampyrus and you gave up your own life – your own species as you were the last of them – so that the Humans and Vampyrus could find their way. That has been your true greatness, Kiera Hudson."

"So what happens to me now?" I asked.

"Because you failed to make your choice, you are now out of the reach of God's blessings. You have been cursed to walk in the shadow of death."

"But I couldn't choose," I cried out. "Your God asked the impossible."

"The decision was made for you," another of the Elders said, its toothless gums rubbing sorely together. "The Hollows have been sealed forever. Those Vampyrus that had made lives for themselves above ground have been snatched back, never to return. All of them will forget about their past lives, just as the humans will forget about them."

"And the war?" I asked.

"The humans will not remember how some parts of their cities fell. As you know all too well, the humans are resourceful and imaginative creatures. They won't be able to explain what happened, but they'll imagine something, they always do."

"Earthquakes, I shouldn't wonder," another of the Elders roared with spiteful laughter.

"And what of me?" I asked them, desperate not to look upon their grotesque wounds and faces.

"You are now one of the living dead," the female said. "Cursed to walk the Earth alive, yet dead."

"You have become one of the Dead Flesh," one of them boomed like thunder. "You have no heart and no soul. You are unable to enter Heaven or Hell. Until..."

"Until what," I begged.

"Until your curse has been lifted," another of them said, its voice growing fainter.

"And how is the curse lifted?"

"We will send three dark angels to guide you," the female said from beneath me as if fading away.

"How will I know who they are?"

"Their names are Malachi, Gabriel, and Uriel," The Elder's voice no more than a distant whisper.

"Where will they guide me to...?" I asked as I gazed into...

Chapter Forty-One

...the eyes of the pathologist. I looked round at the morgue. The policeman was clutching his legs as he lay on the floor screaming. There was another guy in a white lab coat cowering in the corner.

"How did I get here?" I asked the female pathologist, and my face felt odd, as if I had just recovered from some injury.

"I was carrying out a post-mortem on you," she mumbled, as if not believing herself.

"But where did I come from?" I pushed.

"Your body was found up on the mountainside," The police officer screeched in pain. "You shouldn't be alive. You had no face or fingers – you have no *heart*!

"What's he talking about?" I said, looking down at my hands, then, gently touching my face with them.

"It looked as if you had been mauled by some giant wolf," the pathologist told me. "He's right, you were brought here in a body bag, with half your face and fingers missing. But..."

"But what?" I asked.

"They grew back right in front of us," she mumbled as if she were going to cry.

"You're fucking dead!" the police officer roared, in pain and fear. "And now you're walking around the morgue."

Then, staring at me as if I were some interesting medical freak show, the pathologist said, "Who are you? What are you?"

Before I'd the chance to answer her, the mortuary door crashed open and two figures came running in. And it was my turn to look shocked, confused, and bewildered.

"I thought you were dead?" I breathed.

"We were," Isidor said, aiming his crossbow at the police officer lying on the floor.

"Stop pointing that goddamn thing at me, will ya?" the police officer roared. "Can't you see she's busted up my legs?"

Then, turning to the second figure that had come crashing through the door, I said, "Kayla, is that really you?"

Smiling at me, Kayla came forward, and said, "Kiera, what

196

happened to you? You look like shit!"

"Can someone tell me what's going on here?" the pathologist asked, backing away from the three of us.

"I'd like to know the answer to that myself," I breathed, not believing that Kayla and Isidor were standing before me.

"You're alive," I gasped, reaching for them to make sure that they were real.

"No, we're dead!" Isidor said, stepping back towards the door as if preparing to make a quick exit.

"In fact, we're angels," Kayla corrected him.

"I get it," I said as Kayla pulled me towards the door. "They said there would be three of you."

"C'mon, we don't have time," Isidor shouted at me, looking back over his shoulder. "We've got to get out of here – something really bad has happened!"

Before I could ask what, Kayla took my hand and dragged me towards the open door. I looked back at the pathologist and said, "Kiera Hudson."

"Sorry?" she frowned.

"You asked me who I was," I reminded her. "My name is Kiera Hudson, and I'm one of the Dead Flesh."

Then I was gone, racing out into the night after my friends, not looking back.

I followed them to a car, its taillights burning an angry red in the night. There was someone leaning against the side of it, but it was dark and I couldn't see who it was.

Kayla and Isidor raced towards the car as if there was no time to lose, and I raced after them, unable to take my eyes off the figure standing against the car. There was something vaguely familiar about the shape and size of his silhouette and if I'd had a heart, it would have been racing in my chest.

Within feet of the figure I knew who it was, and I raced towards him, throwing myself into his arms.

"Take it easy, tiger," Potter whispered as he held me tight.

"I love you," I whispered back, and he kissed the tears that flowed down my face. Leaning back from his arms so I could look into his eyes, needing to make sure it was really him, I said, "Potter, is it really you?"

But before he'd had a chance to answer, Isidor climbed into the back of the car and as he did, he grinned, "Yeah, it's him alright, except his name isn't Potter anymore, it's Gabriel." Letting go of me, Potter raced around the side of the car, but not quick enough to stop Isidor from slamming the door shut in his face.

"My name is *Potter*!" he shouted through the glass as Isidor grinned back at him. "It's not Gabriel, that's a freaking girl's name!"

"That's what those Elders named you when they brought you back," Kayla reminded him as she winked at me and climbed onto the backseat next to her brother.

"I couldn't give a rat's arse what those old farts called me," Potter barked and stuck a cigarette in the corner of his mouth. "My name's *Potter*, okay?"

"Whatever makes you happy," Isidor smirked from the backseat of the car.

"Can you believe this shit?" Potter moaned at me. "I've been raised from the freaking dead to spend the rest of eternity listening to that wise-arse!"

"Nothing changes you, does it?" I said, looking over the roof of the car at him.

"Listen, sweet-cheeks, it's not me who needs to change," he snapped. "It's that dumb arse." Then, he climbed in behind the steering wheel.

I got in next to him as he fired up the engine and sped out of the car park. Smiling to myself, I watched as he chewed on the cigarette that dangled from the corner of his mouth.

"And that's another thing," Isidor said from the back. "Do you have to smoke all the time?"

"What's the problem?" Potter snapped at him. "It's not as if it's gonna kill ya! You're dead already, you Muppet!"

"But it stinks..." Isidor continued.

Then shooting me a sideways glance, Potter said, "Do me a favour, sweet-cheeks and put the radio on - I've had enough of his whining already."

I switched the radio on, and the car filled with the sound of Coldplay singing *Charlie Brown*.

Settling back into my seat, I made the most of this happy moment, all of us being back together again. Because somewhere inside of me, I got the feeling this happiness wouldn't last for long.

'Dead Flesh'
(Kiera Hudson Series Two)
Book 1
Now Available

More books by Tim O'Rourke

Vampire Shift (Kiera Hudson Series 1) Book 1
Vampire Wake (Kiera Hudson Series 1) Book 2
Vampire Hunt (Kiera Hudson Series 1) Book 3
Vampire Breed (Kiera Hudson Series 1) Book 4
Wolf House (Kiera Hudson Series 1) Book 4.5
Vampire Hollows (Kiera Hudson Series 1) Book 5
Dead Flesh (Kiera Hudson Series 2) Book 1
Dead Night (Kiera Hudson Series 2) Book 1.5
Dead Angels (Kiera Hudson Series 2) Book 2
Dead Statues (Kiera Hudson Series 2) Book 3
Dead Seth (Kiera Hudson Series 2) Book 4
Dead Wolf (Kiera Hudson Series 2) Book 5
Dead Water (Kiera Hudson Series 2) Book 6
Witch (A Sydney Hart Novel)
Black Hill Farm (Book 1)
Black Hill Farm: Andy's Diary (Book 2)
Doorways (Doorways Trilogy Book 1)
The League of Doorways (Doorways Trilogy Book 2)
Moonlight (Moon Trilogy) Book 1
Moonbeam (Moon Trilogy) Book 2
Vampire Seeker (Samantha Carter Series) Book 1